CW01202940

ANGEL

BY K. SPENCER

This book is a work of fiction. All names of characters, places and incidents are products of the authors imagination or are used fictitiously. Not recommended for under 18.

Angel copyright 2016 by K. Spencer. All rights reserved. No part of this book may be used or reproduced in any manner whatsoever without the authors written permission.

Photo copyright 2016 by Focus One Photography

This book is dedicated to my husband and kids. If it wasn't for you this wouldn't have been written. I love you all for being my rocks. To my Bestie James Stewart thank you for pushing me and being there when I was about to lose my mind when I couldn't write. My Beta's thank you for letting me know you loved this book. Reading it and for editing when needed. I know it has taken me a long time to write this, but I had a bit of writers block. Thank you to Katrina Worby for being Angel on the cover you are perfect and I love you loads. To Kate Wooster of Focus One Photography. You are amazing. You captured the perfect picture for the cover. Love you loads and loads. To DJ Kurt thank you so much for allowing me to use your tracks in this book. To Kieran Keyes thank you for allowing me to use Ravers Reunited name in this book. I only ever go to Ravers Reunited events and I love that I was able to bring it in this book. To Bink Cummings, sister I cant thank you enough for the help you have gave me getting this book out. Love you. Thank you to K.E. Osborn for your insight loves ya. And lastly but certainly not least to you, the reader. Knowing that you are about to read this, gives me a massive amount of happiness, that you will read something that took a lot for me to have the courage to write. Enjoy

Yasmine

Happy Reading

Hugs

K. Spencer

TABLE OF CONTENTS

SCOTTISH LINGO

Ye - You

Tae - To

Aff - Off

Hawd - Hold

Yer - Your

Sa - So

CHAPTER 1

Dear Miles

Hi. Never done this whole writing to an inmate thing so don't really know where to start. May as well start about me I guess. Well I'm Scottish live in England. 28 year old raver with 2 children one girl one boy who are my world. Recently single not that it really matters tbh hey ho next well I have tattoos facial piercings wow that doesn't really explain what those piercings are does it. I have what's called angel bites up top and a vertical labret on my bottom lip. As I said I am a raver anything from hardcore through to gabber is what I love to listen to. Favorite rave event would have to be Ravers Reunited the atmosphere is just amazing. I am a barmaid at weekends and during the week I'm all about my kids. Hmmm what else ? Ah why I am writing? Well I thought I would try and brighten someone's day OK I may really just be making you wonder why the hell I'm rambling on about crap and making it seem like I'm a complete weirdo but hey at least you ain't bored right now BONUS hahaha. Well I'm going to go if you want to write awesome if not that's alright.

Yours Claire :)

Dear Claire

Well hello Scottish girl. As you know my name is Miles I hate being called Miles please call me Demon I would rather go by that. Well me I'm a 30 year old biker I'm in an MC I'm also the SAA of the club. I have no kids, never had a steady girl. Have tattoos all over and a piercing although I'm not telling you where, I want you to guess. Never heard hardcore before I'm a rock man myself. You may be wondering why I'm in here, well me and the VP got caught with a gun on our bikes so we both got a year so far we have done 3 months so another 9 to go. I'm guessing you would like to keep in contact so when the time comes I will just give you an address to write to, but, hey you may not even want to chat after a while we will see. And you did brighten up my day although a pic of you would be nice to have so I know what you look like. Well I'm needing to go lights out in about an hour and I'm going to hand this to a guard to send to you.

Hope you write back

Demon

8 Months later

Dear Demon

Well ain't you just a barrel fun on that letter pal! You asked me if I thought I could see us going somewhere all I said was what about the distance? I said I would find out if I could move me and the kids to you. BTW I did and its doable as long as I have somewhere to stay and a job and that I had full custody of the kids which as you know I do. So I don't know where the argument has came from. You haven't even gave me an address I've to write to for fuck sake! Take yer knickers oot yer arse and breathe. I don't want to argue with you. I've had a shitty week and that letter just put the cherry on top. You have a month til your out I need an address. To change the subject as this is just doin my head in! A bit of happy for me i'm going to Ravers Reunited I can't bloody wait wearing a pink outfit I think so need new fluffies aswell. Sitter for the kids is already arranged yay. I love you Demon forever and always.

Love Claire xxxx

I hate having to speak like that, I don't even like when I have to be big bad mummy to the kids. I love being able to give my kids the world but sadly I ain't got a tree that magically gives me money. I work 2 jobs one during the week one at the weekend to support my babies. Their dad isn't in the picture, years of abuse put a stop to that. Let's just say police were called one too often, a hospital trip and the help of women's aid and a really good lawyer helped. Plus his exact words to the court were " I never wanted those bastards" didn't help his case so I moved miles away. Ava is my eldest at 10 and Peter is my youngest at 8. Me im 29. Brown hair to my shoulders usually dyed blonde or red depending on my mood right now its red. Hazel eyes. Size 12 big boobs well to me anyway.

As I get up off the couch to go make a cuppa and finish cleaning the kitchen my eldest walks in. Wearing her normal light blue skinny jeans and a top which currently is my T-shirt. What is it with kids and my clothes? Swear I have a wardrobe that states "Take my contents Mum won't mind" To my eldest but only she can see it. Thankfully that's all getting packed in about 2 weeks. Ava is looking at her tablet when she lifts her head at my throat clearing.

"Mum can I go to Lyndsay's?" Ava asked. Ava is a bit too much like me. Can be temperamental when she wants. She's my brown haired green eyed little Princess. She is pretty determined to succeed in tattooing when she is older but we will see what happens. Whatever she wants to do I will be there every step of the way.

"Sure hunny do you want me to drive you round? Phone me at 4 so I can pick you up for tea, then Stacy is round to watch you and your brother as I'm going out tonight remember. We need to go to Asda to get films and snacks for you two tonight."

"Please mum that would be awesome! Did you say you had the next 2 weeks off to pack everything up? I'm kinda excited to be moving to America. You did sort the school out didn't you?"

Swear you would think I forgot things the way she rattles off lists "Yes Princess I sorted the school out and yesterday was actually my last day as we move in 3 weeks thankfully you both finish school in a week so you can help"

"Mummm do I need to? Can't I just like watch you do it all? " She moans. What is she a teenager? Pretty sure she's 10 not 13!

"Yes you need to I'm not wonder woman you know. Unless you want to move without your room your helping lady"

"OK OK I will help I will help god! Haha love you Mum can you take me now tho? Please?"

Getting up getting my keys. Shouting Peter to come so we can go. All of us in the car I take Ava to Lyndsay's house. "Mum can I get a new game please? I will not ask again until we get settled please mum my last one is finished and the new one is out now" Peter asks so politely and I really can't say no when he does that face. "OK wee man I need to go into town anyway for bits for tonight anyway. Trip to Leicester? "

"Mum I love you I can even see if the new trainers are in" Wait a minute here how did a trip for a game lead to trainers? So glad I've already arranged everything for the move and put money away.

Went home sorted Peter lunch. Started packing up the living room stopped and decided I will do it Monday. Stuff that I've got a night out to get ready for. Had a relaxing bath put the Hardcore on. Mail man arrives and we have our usual chat after he found out from my noisy neighbour I was moving he has been so nice asking if I knew how to go about redirecting my mail. He has helped so much. Now as he drops off the parcel with Peters present for his birthday next month. I can't stop being upset that its been a month since I last heard anything from Demon, I thought he actually loved me. Guess you can't be right all the time. He made me feel things about him I never thought could be real. Guess I'm just a bloody fool. This move was never because of Demon. It is for me and the kids we all want a fresh start. Me and the kids sat down and said we wanted to move where better than Alabama ? OK we did the map finger stop thing but I found work straight a way as a tattooist so yeah that was strangely good. I say strangely as when I said my name he asked me to repeat it, asked if I had any experience obviously I do but still I sent him my resume he emailed me back the next day asking when I was moving.

DEMON

Sitting in the hotel in Leicester in front of my VP Rage and I don't know why the fuck I agreed to this shit. Yeah OK he helped me out replying to this bitch I mean come on I've got an Old Lady at home I only applied to that fucking stupid chat with a new friend because I was bored. Didn't fucking expect someone to reply so Rage has been chatting to her and he like a dumb fuck has fallen for the bitch!

"Demon are you ready to help me here she needs to come with us she is gonna be my Old Lady and she is going to blow up when the truth comes out that she ain't been talking to you" shaking my head I sigh "Yeah brother I got you I will do what it takes "

"Hot fucking damn VP you seen her Facebook lately. Fuck me if the bitches over here are dressed like her I'm going to fall fucking hard for a few" Teeth shouts from the other room, yeah I can see this being one of those nights.

RAGE

"Hot fucking damn VP you seen her Facebook lately. Fuck me if the bitches over here are dressed like her I'm going to fall fucking hard for a few" Teeth shouts .

Gritting my teeth its hard not to go punch him in the teeth. What the fuck is he looking at Claire's pictures for?

"Get off her page asshole. She is my Old Lady show some fucking respect ! I swear any of you lot fuck this up and heads will fucking roll. Demon thanks for this brother when she is home I will put my name on her cutt. Teeth I know what she looks like in her pictures I have fucking got photos from her stay off her page asshole not telling you again. Let's get ready brothers we have 30 minutes to go see my Old Lady. Crank no fucking any bitches at this thing get your dick wet at home brother" He ain't happy but tough shit.

I head to the bathroom to get ready. Leaning against the sink I think this can't go wrong its going to feel horrible seeing my brother touching and kissing Claire but when we are back home I will sit her ass down and explain and hopefully she doesn't walk the fuck away cause that shit ain't going to happen no fucking way will I allow that shit! She's mine. Slipping my black jeans and my white wife beater on I walk out the bathroom walking past the laptop I see my Old Lady in a pink bra with flowers and shit all over it a fucking pink tutu that barely covers her ass. White hot rage fills me. Yeah her ass is being tanned good. Tonight when I fuck her she's getting her ass smacked. What the fuck does she think she's wearing?

"Hey Teeth see if she will add me on here will ya? Want to see if she has written anything, she probably won't add me but worth a fucking try" Shouting through to him while he is getting another beer from the fridge.

"Bro just click add friend its as easy as that" He is looking at me as if I'm a fucking idiot.

"This is your Facebook not mine bro not adding her to yours dickhead" I state.

"Its your fucking account VP add her for fuck sake" he snorts

"What you doing on my account stop fucking doing this shit I hate when you log in to the brothers accounts" growling at him he knows we hate this shit!

Laughing at me "Fuck bro don't use a shit password then"

Clicking the add friend button I finish getting ready.

CHAPTER 2

CLAIRE

Standing in line having a smoke. Seeing Mizz-T giving her a massive hug not seen this girl in about 6 months and knowing its going to be the last time kinda brings a tear to my eye. But she's told me she will keep in touch that's really all my friends have said not that they would come see me which OK is kinda sad but it ain't cheap getting to America. Finishing my smoke I'm let in. Straight to the dancefloor stomping to Concrete Angel. Turned on the flashing lights on my fluffies stomping for a good 20 mins I shoot off to the bar order a blue vk and a shot of vodka I get back on the floor enjoying the atmosphere, seeing so many of my mates and thinking I'm going to miss this. And then think but I'm starting a new phase of mine and the kids lives. After 2 hours in the main room I go to listen to Mizz-T set and its absolutely banging I love her.

You ever had that feeling of someone staring at you yeah? I'm feeling it but shrug it off. Another half hour and I go upstairs for a smoke. Get to the top of the stairs spark up while messaging Stacy to see how the kids are when I hear

"Well brothers my Old Lady is one sexy bitch"

A deep American voice that sends shivers down my spine and makes my panties wet drawls behind me. I freeze not knowing what to do. Do I slap him? Do I climb him like a pole ? Do I even turn around ? No! I just pull up the camera and selfie the bastard with my tongue out. Hey first pic has to be done. I feel heat behind me and smell leather from his cut I close my eyes and just breathe.

Taking a deep breath I turn and look up. He has to be at least 6'5 muscles everywhere brown hair tied up in a bandana. Deep blue eyes and tattoos everywhere. Damn my panties are soaking wet and I just want him now!

"Hi Demon how are you? Enjoying being out of jail? Yeah that's something I wouldn't know now is it since I ain't heard a fucking word from you. What the fuck are you doing here? And I ain't your Old Lady you fucked that up when I didn't hear a fucking word from you. Now if you don't mind kindly fuck off back home" I rage at him.

How fucking dare he even attempt this shit. "Claire I'm fine thanks actually no. I'm fucking perfect now. I ain't gonna apologise so get that right out your head now ain't ever going to happen. You are my Old Lady so get used to it. Now get that fine ass over here and give your Old Man a kiss. Think I deserve it for not kicking asses so far." With a smug look he waits. I smile ever so slowly walk up and walk straight past him back to the main room. Fuck that shit he can apologize and fucking grovel at my feet.

He is 2 steps behind me and I shiver knowing it. Straight to the bar I need a drink I order a pint and down it like its a cool glass of water. He's next to me he grabs me lifts me to his face and lands a kiss. He licks my bottom lip making me gasp as I do his tongue starts to intertwine with mine. Fuck me that's a kiss and I can't help but wrap my legs around him. His hands are on my ass. Kneading the globes.

I come up for air and he whispers in my ear "Fuck Claire I need you! Your my Old Lady. I'm gonna ink you and put a ring on you. You and my kids are my world come home now I ain't asking I'm telling you your all coming home" knowing its the best I'm gonna get that's even close to an apology I say

 "Fine Demon but we are moving in 3 weeks to Alabama I don't even know where you are from! I have a house and a job set up the kids start school after the summer. What we gonna do?"

 A smirk appears on his face as well as his friends " Baby we live where your moving to"

" What?" I shriek

 " Yeah was fucking fate you sexy bitch your mine!"

Talk about fate being a smart bitch! I never actually knew where Demon lived, he never told me that in his letters. All I could do was wrap myself around him and enjoy being near him. Someone accidentally knocked into us, its a rave it happens. Apologies were made by both the guy and me as you do. You can't help knocking into each other everyone is stomping your body goes where it goes at a rave.

"I'm going for a pee will be 2 mins babe" I shout to Demon

"Want a drink baby?" Demon asks me while staring straight at my tits. Rolling my eyes "Yeah bottle of water babe please" I head off to the toilet Demon stops me "Put this on baby your claimed, time to show it" I take the leather look at the back on it there's the club symbol and of the bottom it says "Property of" looking at him and he is staring at me eyebrow raised and waits til I slide it on. The look on his face is pure satisfaction. Yeah I think to myself just you wait til we get home that look will be on my face as I scream your name buddy! Wow my man is hot no he's more than hot don't think theres a word that covers it.

After going to the toilet I hear DJ Kurt come on and I'm back to stomping my heart out. MC Wotsee is on the mic and the set is amazing. After that set

I'm off for a smoke and a check on the kids and to let Stacy know I will probably be home after another set. All I can think is I want to get back so the kids can meet Demon.

"Hey gorgeous, how you feeling ? Gotta introduce you babe. This is my VP Rage this here is Teeth and Crank. Brothers this is Claire my Old Lady"

Rage is the same height as Demon pretty much the same build but has a scar running down his face from his eye to his jaw on the left side, has sandy blonde hair and green eyes. Teeth has a goofy smile on his face and is about 6ft pretty looks like he works out. Crank well he's just a baby face but looks like a rugby player. All of them together pretty intimidating.

"Hi how are you all? Babe why are you here? How are you here? Where are you staying?" I question him.

He wraps his big strong arms around me and says "Baby why I am here is simple I'm helping you come home. How I am here is also simple I boarded a plane" smirk definitely on his face.

"Don't be a smart ass babe" I growl at him.

"We are at a hotel but tomorrow if you have space we will move into your house til we move. I want to meet my kids tomorrow babe and take everyone for dinner."

"No I don't think so I'm good with everything but dinner the kids want macaroni cheese and you will eat it the lot of you will no exceptions Demon what the kids want they get. Wee mans birthday is in a month and we will only be in the new house a week then, and I'm not bringing my furniture or my car so its just the bits and pieces and they are being sent in 2 weeks and they will arrive when we do. We are only bringing a suitcase on the plane. So you lot can help pack up the house." I tell him with a frown on my face.

"OK babe OK no dinner but packaged Mac and cheese what the hell? "

"It ain't packaged its home made so correct yourself please" I say.

Growled into my ear he says "Keep talking like that and you are gonna find your ass red and my dick in it" Holy shit talk about do I don't I! I need to get this man home I can't get any wetter.

"Claire hun any chance we can hurry this up I need to check in with the Pres" says Rage. He is giving me a look that screams hurry the fuck up.

"Yeah I will have this smoke then go for a pee then we can get your stuff from the hotel unless u just want to get it tomorrow"

" Get that shit tomorrow I need food though" replies Crank.

So we all leave and its kind of the end of me raving well it feels it. We get into the taxi and we get food knowing my kids are probably still up since its Stacy watching them I grab them a pizza. We start the drive to my house. Pulling up I see the living room light on and that Peters light is still on. Can't see Ava's as her room is at the back. We get out the taxi and open the front door.

Hearing laughter in the living room I open the door to see a sea of popcorn. "Is this how we live when mum ain't home? Nope pretty sure it ain't. We have guests kids ones you need to get to know. So kindly clean it up pizza will be sorted in 2 minutes." Yeah I was totally kidding it wasn't actually that bad but still I hate mess.

"Baby its only a popcorn fight calm down" my jaw drops is he serious? My kids know I'm kidding and I know the second I walk through that door I'm being attacked by popcorn.

"Yep I know just wait. Can you bring the box and the pop please babe." I give him a kiss that gets hotter the longer I kiss him. I have to drag myself away or my next door neighbour is gonna have a sight to see.

Walking into the living room I'm bombarded with popcorn and as Demon and the boys are a step behind they get it too. I get to my chair to safety and call time-out. "Right kids the tall one next to me is Demon. Can you remember me telling you about him? The guy I was writing to in jail? This is him. Mums new boyfriend I guess you'd call him."

"Old Man husband etc get this right babe your mine these kids are mine. Yeah kids you can either call me Demon or dad whichever you like" Yeah alpha male has arrived.

Ava's head shoots round. I can see the argument starting now "Ava don't. I know you ain't wanting to call him dad I know you will be thinking he's being a twat but think before you speak. I don't tolerate ignorance in my house. You know this young lady if you want to say something you know to say it in private"

" But mum I can't call him dad I will stick to Demon not dad I don't even know him." Ava states. "Mum he has tattoos and looks kinda scary and what's with the leather is he like the men you tattoo? How come he has a nickname and I can't? That's not fair. Does he drive a bike? Can he show me how to drive? Does he have kids?" My little inquisitive Peter asks.

"Ava he ain't moving in not yet anyway but you will be seeing a lot of him. I would like you to like him so can you at least try for me? He ain't a bad man I can promise you that" I look at Demon hoping that I'm right. " Peter no nicknames your friends can call you what they like me not a chance. He does look scary but he's a good guy and yes he's like the men I tattoo yes he rides a bike no you won't be getting on a bike ever! And no he doesn't have kids. Any other questions?" I raise an eyebrow and wait. Not one peep out the room.

"Mum OK I will call him Demon. Hi Demon my names Ava. Mum I will try but I ain't promising its gonna happen quick but I will try for you. Oh I was looking in Amazon and saw the best ever princess bed can I have it for my new room I want the biggest room you said I could have a big room you promised" And that's my Ava can be moody one minute and its like a switch she remembers what she has seen she wants and the world breathes a sigh of relief.

"Ava can we get over there first I will have a look and see if it is nice til then wait. Now I'm having a cuppa eating my pizza then we will finish watching this then we go bed as its a busy day and I need this house done these guys are helping" Getting up Ava rushes to me and cuddles me. I get my tea settle down finishing everything I head to bed with Demon following shouting night to everyone.

Demon heads to the toilet while I strip for bed wearing a sexy black see through babydoll with a pull rope in the front that just covers my bum. Just as I get into bed the light goes off and I'm plunged into darkness. OK maybe he doesn't like to fuck with the lights on weird but oh well. I feel the bed dip with his weight and he slowly runs his hand around my left leg and tugs it wider to give him access to my slick pussy. Oh so slowly he runs his tongue along the inside of my leg and I'm feeing like my body is going to explode if he doesn't lick my pussy soon. A sharp pain has me gasping an pulling away, fucking bastard just bit my inner thigh what the actual fuck! He grabs my leg and kisses where he bit me. Then begins to lick the rest of the way to my pussy instantly my body bows as he forces his tongue deep into my glistening hole.

It's relentless I can hardly take a breath as he just wont stop his aggressive tongue lashing. All of a sudden he stops flips me on my stomach and pins me flat to the bed slapping my ass hard. "Ow what the fuck Demon" He slaps my ass harder then slams his massive cock in me and relentlessly drills into me harder and harder im biting my pillow to stop from screaming out with the force of my orgasm, just as I peak through my orgasm I hear him grunting as he cums in me, I begin floating back down into my body. Trying to catch my breath with a massive smile on my face. "I love you Demon I'm still pissed with you but I love you." Passing out cuddled up to him my last thought is we didn't use protection.

CHAPTER 3

CLAIRE

7 WEEKS LATER

We have arrived at the new house a nice 4 bedroom 2 bathrooms downstairs toilet massive living room and a heavenly kitchen dining room I love my new house its gorgeous white with pale green shutters a massive front and back garden. While I've not bought a car yet I am looking as we are basically in the countryside and its an hour walk to the town and a taxi back when we did our first full shop which is a pain in the ass.

Demon went back 3 days after arriving as something happened at the club. I haven't heard a peep which has pissed me off. How can he just not get in contact with me at all. He's so hot and cold I'm beginning to think fuck him he can stay clear of me from now on. The kids are happily lazing in the sun. Peter has asked for a dog and I told him that sadly its a no not right now maybe in a few months when we are settled.

Just as I'm cutting vegetables for dinner my phone rings "Hello?" A voice I haven't heard in about 2 years answers.

 "Hi Angel. How are you?"

I'm stunned and slightly worried "Hi Uncle Graham I'm good kids are good I'm guessing you know I've moved. How are you and why are you calling? I'm no longer in your business so this I'm hoping is just a call to see how your god daughter and her kids are and not asking a favour I'm not in Britain anymore!" I couldn't keep it nice I just couldn't he maybe my god father but for no contact in 2 years he can just fuck right off unless its serious if its serious and to do with business he and I both know I will do what I can.

A long sigh comes through the line " Angel please don't be like this you are the one who left and, I totally agree but you never left a number, I'm only just getting it. I know you live in Alabama and I really didn't want to ask this but you are the only one I trust to deal with this. If after what I tell you, you want to say fuck off and not deal then I will send my men but please just listen to it all" Taking a giant breath I agree to listen and I get angrier and angrier at what I'm hearing

"I will deal with it what's the number and other details"

"Thank you Angel I will send you everything you need in an email to your old account do you need anything?" He is being my Uncle again and I don't blame him god help the fucking fanny who has pissed me off and that name would be Canyon Devils MC right here in my new town.

"Yeah I need a car if you can get one here by tomorrow preferably something fast and if you can something that I would drive normally please I will phone the clubhouse with the number you call which by the sounds is the bar. Send me the details asap please the faster I sort this the better!" I can hear his smile through the phone

"Angel a Mustang is on its way to you now details are sent if you need anything or if you want the boys sending, which I highly doubt I will send them. Give the kids a kiss from me and I love you all thank you for doing this"

"Love you too I'm going to finish making dinner and shout the kids in will phone you tomorrow once I've seen to it" Hanging up I seethe. Oh hell fire is going to rain down and I'm the instrument to do it. Its been nearly 10 years since I've done work for the family and right now its coursing through me in hot waves. I was an enforcer for my family and when I had Ava I couldn't do it anymore. I've been through a bunch of shit and pulled into myself for years. Yeah no more no one fucks over my family. I will get the kids fed and put to bed then I'm going to phone the clubhouse and talk to their Pres and see what the fuck his game is.

Ava and Peter come flying through the back door shouting for food which is officially sorted both look happy if they are happy I'm happy now to sit them down and drop the bomb I'm going out tomorrow night.

"Kids I've got Selene coming tomorrow night to watch you for a few hours. I won't be long I just need to do a few things." Ava looks at me and says "OK mum don't do anything I wouldn't" she has a big smile on her face and I can't help but smile at her sassy little Princess just like her mummy. Peter is happily eating and nodding his head another day in the Miller household.

A few hours later a nice shiny mustang is sitting in my drive with the reg plate BL4DZ damn I've missed that plate !! Uncle Graham came through for me big time. Kids are sleeping have been for 2 hours. Picking up the phone and thinking shit here we go. I've got one of my old blades in my hand flipping it.

I dial the clubhouse. "Hello" taking a deep breath I reply "Hey I need to talk to your Pres its important"

A giant hard done to sigh comes through the line "Fucking hell what is it with you fucking English people that's everyday for the last 2 weeks. What cause the guy ain't getting no answer they send a bitch to phone Pres ain't interested now fuck off!"

 Rage pours off me in waves who the fuck does this bitch think she's talking to?? "Here idiot don't dare speak to me like that give you a hint either get your Pres or pass a message on which is it?" I hear a click.

Oh hell fucking no! Seems it was a good thing I got selene to watch the kids tomorrow. I'm going to have so much fun with that stupid bitch. Quickly sending my Uncle an email I head to my bed flopping down thinking of what I need to do tomorrow gives me a shiver and to be honest nah not a good one. Since the kids have went bed I've been throwing blades it calmed me down and as usual I ain't missed a damn target so at least I ain't rusty.

Wakening up the next morning I get the kids ready to go to town for a new outfit for tonight. Knowing that I have at least 2 blades I need to cover as the rest will be in plain sight or to me they will as they are the easier ones to get too. And I can actually see them helps there to everyone else they look like jewelry.

"Mum what's wrong?" Turning my head I look at Peter that boy can read me like a book sometimes "Nothing wee man just trying to find something that's me but can help me blend in so I don't look stupid"

"Where you going mum"

"A biker bar sweetheart so I don't want to look horrid" tilting his head he says "How about your red dress and black boots you look pretty in that."

With a big smile I hug him and say "What would I do without you wee man"

"You'd be lost mummy, lost!" So true is my boy so true.

7pm I'm in my car and driving to the clubhouse knowing that not only will Demon be there but if this isn't sorted shit is gonna hit the fan and hit it hard. I'm in a red salsa dress with black knee high boots with a 5 inch heel hair is up in a curled up do with curls at either side of my face make up is smokey eyes false eyelashes and pinky red lips. I feel sexy yet with all 24 blades yeah you heard right 24 blades and only 6 are hidden I also feel like the old me is back the one I lost all those years ago. Why I allowed a man to treat me like shit I will never know.

Driving into the clubhouse I see men and women all around a few stare at my car probably wondering who the fuck I am. Well they are about to find out. After allowing the car to cool down I switch the engine off grab my bag and slowly step out of the car I can feel eyes on me and that's exactly what I want. Shutting the car and pressing the lock and alarm button I make my way to the building where I know the officers of the club are it is a bar after all.

I pull my phone out open the door and dial the bar "Hello" says the bitch at the bar hearing the same voice.

I smirk "Hi there doll fancy getting your Pres for me please" seeing this bitch roll her eyes put her hand on her hip and say "Fuck off you English cunt" interrupting her I smile and say

"I'm Scottish doll not English bit of a difference there now kindly get your Pres business needs discussing" as I say this I'm walking to the bar when she replies I'm right in front of her

" Bitch I ain't getting him he has enough women in his life he certainly doesn't need you. You fucking Scottish bitch! Now fuck off and stop calling" she slams the phone down fluffs her hair and I just wave my phone at her.

Grabbing her head I slam it down on the bar hey I avoided the glasses. "Hi doll note to self for ya don't ever call me a cunt or a bitch now where is your Pres."

At this moment in time I see something out the corner if my eye that causes pure and utter heartbreak and with that comes utter fucking hatred!

Let's backtrack to this morning I'm sitting in the bathroom staring at the pregnancy test and thinking well shit baby number 3 on the way was a bloody shocker. As I'm on the pill and have been for 6 years. But back to the hatred and heartbreak.

On the pool table in the middle of the fucking room is Demon fucking some woman. Slowly releasing the tramp I have hold of I tell her to get me the Pres and she scurries off to do as I ask. Leaning against the bar I at least wait til the piece of shit finishes when he looks up and spots me his face is no expression but I know he must be wondering why I'm here.

I stroll up to him and say "Oh hi Demon, sorry I would have came over sooner but you were busy may as well let you know you're going to be a daddy congratulations! I will let you know when my child is born then you can decide if you want anything to do with him or her. Got to go as I'm waiting to discuss something with one of your officers" just as I say this the woman he was fucking on the table laughs and says

"Oh hunny I doubt my old man has got you pregnant you must be out of your mind he doesn't sleep around on me"

"Bitch your an idiot that wasn't me who fucked you" What the fuck ?!"That wasn't even me who you were talking too. You really are a fucking clueless bitch" Demon sneers.

The two of them walk off laughing. What? So who slept with me ? Who fucked me and got me pregnant. As I'm thinking this I look across the room and spot Rage the VP and across from him is the Pres Lucius. Sitting in the furthest corner grabbing a 2inch blade I throw it across the room to land in the middle of the table and land it does. Smashing through a glass with Bladez written on both sides just so this club knows who they are about to fuck with. An uproar goes off at the table while I saunter over with a sway to my hips and slide in next to Rage.

He sits stunned "Claire what are you doing here ? Shit just went down you need to go" smiling I look straight at him pull out one of my blades and start flipping it

. Turning my head to the Pres "Welll ain't you a hard man to get hold of" raising an eyebrow I continue " Now that I have your attention fancy explaining to me why you think its appropriate to ignore my Uncles phone calls. Yeah you really need to keep in contact with your supplier of guns and drugs. Now you've pissed him off not only do you owe a cool mill, you have me involved and that just pisses me off, although to be honest I would love to find out which of your men got me fucking pregnant, cos according to Demon it definitely was not him. So who the fuck came into my room and fucked me when I thought it was Demon. Never mind that who was I writing too?"

Rage looks at me with his mouth hanging open and a really scary look in his eyes and just won't stop.

 Lucius stares then says "What the fuck! You come into my club hit one of my whores and make demands of me! Little girl you may want to walk before damage to you and yours happens"

At that I start giggling then full out laughing until I have tears streaming down my face. Getting ahold of my self I look at him still half giggling "Oh sweetheart give me a reason to tell my Uncle, that I will happily deal with what needs done. I can happily defend my house from people who think they can threaten my kids I dare you! All you need to do is answer a simple question. Why has my Uncle not been paid? If its a good enough reason I will make a plan with you and we can deal with it if it ain't, well you will see what happens when people threaten my family pal."

Looking at me with a look of respect "We have a problem in the club and we are dealing with it. Your Uncles money was stolen or at least half of it was we still have the other half. I tried calling him and was told he was dealing with a call by his second in command. I hadn't heard from him since so I don't know where you are getting I'm ignoring him"

" Did you get told I had phoned? And I will help deal with the stolen money as it does belong to my Uncle. We need a day where we can sit down and discuss this without ears listening. That is important. Now I'm going to need either your personal number or someone you fully trusts number to contact you tomorrow afternoon and you and your trusted man will come to mine once my kids are asleep and we can discuss what needs to be done to clean up this shitstorm, cos if I come back here I am going to go through the men who were at my house and find out who fucked me when I thought it was Demon. Do we have an agreement tomorrow night at mine?"

 Looking directly at me Lucius shakes my hand takes and says he will be there as well as Rage, who to be honest is freaking me out with the staring. I bid them good night and head home feeling sick to my stomach. Who the fuck did I sleep with? Is that classed as rape? For my own sanity I'm going to not think about it. I'm going to just think of my baby as a miracle. The only good thing to come from this clusterfuck is my baby think of the positive Claire think of the positive. Getting home I phone my Uncle and let him know what's happening telling him that I would pay the other half ensued an argument but I told him to use the money from one of the nightclubs that I co own which he grudgingly agrees to but says from now on any and all deals must go through me, oh how much fun is that I'm a fucking middle man.

Never mind the fact I'm back in the fold as an enforcer how did this happen again? I need my bed I'm shattered so I trudged upstairs to my bed. Just as I feel myself drift I hear the roar of a motorcycle coming into my garden I shoot straight up grab my 9mm and open the window and point at the biker who turns out to be Rage.

"We need to talk now!"

"Ha! No I'm going to bed my kids are asleep and I'm tired and going to sleep goodnight Rage" shutting my window I go back to bed and promptly pass the fuck out.

CHAPTER 4

Wakening up feeling like a truck has ran over me I grudgingly get out my bed. Make my way through the hall to the kitchen for a much needed cuppa I walk into a fucking disaster

"What the hell is happened to my kitchen? KIDS GET IN HERE NOW!!!!" Roaring at the top of my lungs. I hear the kids barrelling downstairs and into the kitchen.

"What the hell is this mess? How many times do I have to tell you that you clean up after yourselves? Its really not that bloody hard to do!"

Peter shifts looking down at his feet and I know I'm about to feel like utter shit I just know it, its in his eyes that are so watery and heartbreaking "Mum did you not see the plate next to your bed? I made you a card and everything you always go to your phone to check the time, and that was on the table so I put the plate there about 5 minutes ago. I went to ask Ava if she could help clean as I made a mess, and she was getting dressed so I waited in my room for her. Sorry for the mess mummy"

Well shit! Now I feel like the worlds worst mother "Sorry baby boy, I didn't see the plate. How about we all go up and eat it then I will come down and clean but you need to help too. Then we can go chill out in the garden? I didn't mean to lose my temper I'm just a bit yucky today which is something I need to talk to you both about. I'm OK before you both start its just something that needs to be discussed well actually there's a few things we need to talk about which will be done today. Upstairs." Ava and Peter both look at each other with an expression of doom.

Going upstairs to my room, we all sit on my bed and start eating Peters pancakes and strawberries with a chocolate sauce I say sauce I actually mean that its swimming in it but I digress. I'm totally going to eat it even if I'm going to get those horrid sugar sweats.

Looking at both kids who keep looking at me with trepidation I say in my softest voice " Kids I'm pregnant. Not only that but there's something I hoped I would never have to tell you, and I understand if you get angry about what I'm about to tell you. Just listen to everything I'm about to say before asking your questions please." Both nodding although they both have whopping big smiles one their faces. I continue knowing this has to be done. I try to make sure the kids know what's happening in our lives. I was told everything in my family so I always said that my kids had the right to know everything.

Taking a deep breath and staring both kids in the eyes I continue to speak "When I turned 12. I found out about the family business. My Uncle is the head of our family and he is a ruthless man. What I'm about to tell you goes no further than us. Is that clear?" Both nod their heads looking a bit apprehensive. "Our family runs the guns and drugs trade. My Uncle who is also my godfather, he is the head of the family. He made me an enforcer when I turned 13. I was a very angry child. And he saw something in me that he wanted to keep trained and ready for his use. Whenever someone didn't pay, me and his other enforcer at the time would deal with it. Now Marc the other enforcer was handy with his fists and guns as well as torture. Me I was trained in hand to hand and knifes. Now when I had you Ava, I told my Uncle that I was stepping away to have you and to raise you. I never wanted my children raised the way I was. I never wanted you both around that environment. But my Uncle has phoned and asked me to sort something, which aye I agreed to do it. I'm not a vicious person but when it comes to family sometimes nothing on this earth will stop you from doing it.

The Canyon Devils MC have refused to either call or answer the phone when my Uncle phoned and they owe him a million dollars for product. He has asked me to deal with it. I agreed under the stipulation that I tell you both about the family business but we keep you out of it. I will NEVER want either of you involved in the family business ever. I will not have you both raised the way I was its not a life I want for you both. I want you to go to college university anything you both want to do I will stand behind you. I want you both to think long and hard about what I have said and if you have any questions do not hesitate to ask as I will answer any and all questions. Now as I said I understand if you both are angry, trust me when I found out I was not a happy bunny. Ask any questions that you have now, now babies and I will answer."

Looking at them both with an eyebrow raised Ava asks "Mum have you ever killed someone?" Her face was scared. "Baby girl I have never killed anyone cut them up aye that was a thing I couldn't ever avoid but I have never ever killed someone."

Peter picking at his shoes asked " With Dad why if you could do this enforcer thing did you let him hurt you? Why not just hurt him back? Why wasn't your Uncle there to help us? Is Dad in that kind of family" Hearing the tears in Peter almost broke me. Taking a deep breath grabbing them both for a cuddle I say " Baby with your dad I didn't and still to this day don't know why I allowed him to do what he has done to us. When it was happening to me I took it as in my head I was making sure he would never do it to you. It was never in my mind to hurt him back and I honestly don't know why. My Uncle never knew until we left and I asked him to leave it be, as I didn't see the point and anything that would happen to him would likely fall back on me. And oh no no no your dad ain't in that kind of family. His is just a normal family baby."

Looking at my kids thinking that they are taking this better than I thought they would Ava pipes up with "Can you train us to use knifes since we kind of are your protégés? And that way it's that fighting skill you wanted us both to learn. You said we had to have a sport a defense and a musical instrument. That's what you said mum. And by the way I'm not sharing my room with my baby brother or sister." I can't help it I burst out laughing! "Oh Ava Bear you do know how to cheer me up! I will think about the knife training, its not something I ever wanted you both to know never mind learn but if you want I will seriously consider it. And hell no you ain't sharing a room I will never hear the end of it."

"Mum is this, what you're doing, going to hurt our baby brother or sister?" Peter asks so softly.

"Oh no baby. I will never let this harm you, your sister or this baby or me for that matter. They don't call me Bladez for nothing you know baby. My family will always be safe. I love all 3 of you so much." By this I've got a single tear running down my face. I can't believe that he would ever think I would allow harm to come to them. Hell will open before that ever happens. Plus the kids have never known what safe guards I have for them.

For the rest of the day we just relax around the house. I've told the kids that Lucius and someone else was coming tonight and they agreed that they would actually go to sleep when I ask them. I will be bloody amazed if they do they are pretty excited about the baby coming. As 8pm comes around I send the kids off to bed receiving my cuddles off them both they go to bed shouting night to the baby. About half 9 my phone pings with a message.

"Claire me and Rage will be there in 45 min. Lucius."

Well then I need a cuppa badly before they appear.

CHAPTER 5

A roar is all I can hear coming towards the house, and I know its Lucius and Rage appearing. Hearing a light tapping on my door I get up to answer walking past my computer I see I have an email. I answer the door to seriously pissed off men. Shrugging my shoulders I let them in "Go sit in the living room its straight through, do you want a drink?"

Rage looks at me as if that's a seriously stupid question "Yeah that's what we want. Beer"

What the ....? Wow here was me being polite too. "In the kitchen I ain't your maid. Until you use your manners thanks" I return with snark.

He turns to walk away saying over his shoulder "Just get us a beer Claire we ain't in the mood for a bitch to bitch to us"

My jaw hits the floor. Who the hell does he think he is? Going to the computer I open the email.

From: Uncle Graham

Phone me when they arrive. I've sent Marc will tell you why when you call. He will arrive in 2 days. He will not be living with you.

No no no I really don't want to see Marc I can just see the arguments.

18 years old

"Hey gorgeous"

Hearing Marc say that gives me shivers. The man is all alpha just the way I like him.

Turning round I see him standing in the doorway muscles straining his suit. He slowly strips his jacket off and my eyes can't look away, my whole body is flushed knowing what is under those clothes. A six pack that feel amazing under my nails every inch of him is pure muscle and strength. Arms that are as thick as a tree thighs that go for hours and a thick and long cock. This man is mine and I thank god daily for him. He is sex personified he has deep blue eyes that see into my very soul, a square jaw a Greek nose and a goatee that feels fucking amazing between my legs.

"Hey sexy, coming to say goodnight? Or did you want something?" My voice comes out breathy and sultry knowing that Marc is about to fuck me into next year. He is 5 years older than me but oh does he have stamina he fucks me for hours and I could do with that tonight.

"We need to talk babe. And you need to sit down" he says with a sigh.

"Babe I got my girl pregnant. And this between us needs to stop. I know you never knew about my girl she's never known about what I do and I ain't gonna tell her. But this, us, is done. Sorry babe."

I'm stunned. My mouth moves like a fish. Then I calmly say "Nice to know I was your slut Marc really ! Noted this is done. Leave before I say something we both won't like. Congratulations on being a dad. True colours shine bright will see you at work next week. " Oh how I wish I could shout and scream maybe even kick the sorry piece of shit in the balls but nope got to be nice as all I was to him was a slag slut whatever you want to call it.

"Claire I'm .." Cutting him off with a look.

"Marc don't even I ain't in the mood you got what you wanted from me and for my Uncles sake I'm going to be nice. Just go home to your family. I'm just going to bed I have a lot to do tomorrow and you really need to fucking leave"

Taking a massive deep breath he turns and leaves. For a year we have been fucking each other and not once did I know he had a girl.

4 days later I walk into my Uncles house ready to sort a few problems when I see Marc all over a blonde while they sit in the office. Squaring my shoulders I walk in head held high walking past them on the black leather couch that should sit 3 people yeah I ain't sitting near them. I walk over the fluffy white rug to my Uncles massive oak table and stop right in front of my Uncle and state " I'm off for a fortnight I have a few things to deal with I need to go to the doctors I don't feel right which

means I'm gonna be aff my game and we can't have that!"

My Uncle looks up and agrees. Not looking at the happy couple I walk straight out the door to my Subaru Impreza this car is a beast and my baby she's decked out to the nines she's sky blue with gold rims she purrs like a tiger and drives like a dream. Time to look out for my happiness.

Present

Since then Marc and I couldn't get along. We constantly argued although that may have been because when he found out that his girls baby wasn't his, my exact words were "wow shocker who knew she was a slag" which in turn caused one hell of an argument where we both walked away with a few cuts and bruises.

Walking into my living room seeing that both men are in my chairs and ready to conduct business I about turn to go to the kitchen to get them beers and me a glass of ice water. As I walk into the living room I hear "this ain't the way to sort this Pres we need a few of our trusted men to help. She can't do this herself. She's pregnant with my kid for fuck sake"

What the hell ? Growling I can't help but grate out through my teeth "Your kid? You wrote to me then didn't have the balls to fucking just come oot with it ? Are you fucking serious right now? Be glad we have shit to sort here or you'd be feeling my fucking blades you piece of shit!"

"Ah shit, Claire Bear don't say shit like that specially to me cos I will take you over my knee and smack that smart little ass. I refuse to allow you to do what needs to be done. Your my Old Lady time to fucking get used to that! "

Hell no I ain't putting up with that shit. Who the hell does this twat think he is? "You best rethink what your ass just spouted because all I heard what utter shite pal. As for your 'allow' wow really? You think you have any right to tell me what to do? I DONT FUCKIN KNOW YOU BAWBAG SA GET THAT

IDEA TAE FUCK!" Walking back through to my kitchen I grab much needed chocolate and try to calm down. Hearing someone walk into the kitchen behind me, taking a deep breath I swear I can smell his rage behind me.

"Look I know you think you don't know me Claire, if that's the case then fine we will start all over again but listen and listen fucking well. YOU are my Old Lady time to act the fucking part get off your high fucking horse and apologise to me in front of my Pres NOW! We will discuss this tomorrow when you have fully calmed down. Until then get your sexy little ass in that room and apologise to me properly and we will discuss what needs discussing for your Uncle." Slapping my ass he herds me to my living room. I'm in near tears. How can he say that shit and expect me to keep together. Do I want to do this with him? Can I ever trust him? Yeah OK maybe for him to save face I should apologise.

"I'm sorry for snapping and losing my temper Rage but after hearing that, well it didn't help and I'm sorry" I say this while looking at my feet, hey I can play the pitiful woman and play it well. As when he appears tomorrow he's getting both barrels.

Rage looks directly at me and growls "Don't do it again Claire."

Lucius looks like he knows shit it going to hit the fan tomorrow with a smirk on his face. " OK Claire we have a feeling you are not going to like this. Not only do we have a piece of scum stealing from us in our chapter but and I'm sorry to say this you also have someone in your organization who has been helping him"

My jaw hits the floor. Adrenaline courses through me. I grab my phone and call Uncle Graham. "Hello gorgeous Neice of mine. How are you Angel? How's the kids? Did you get my email? If you did I'm guessing I also have the grace of the Pres and someone he trusts."

Snickering at the questions "Hey Uncle Graham. I'm about as good as I'm going to get since I'm pregnant again and the father is in the room yes. Kids are fine were a bit shocked with what I told them but that was to be expected. Email received not happy about it but I will be nice. And yep you have that Pres and Rage in the room. Care to tell me who our traitor is? And if you don't know then find out please."

Silence ensues. Now when Uncle Graham goes quiet I get nervous. He is scary when he is quiet its like a sheet of pure calm just envelopes him. "Pardon Angel? Did you just say what I heard you say?"

Lucius clears his throat and says " Mr Miller its Lucius we have had Intel telling us that someone from my club along with someone from your organization has stolen half a mill from us now as I said to your Neice .."

Uncle Graham cuts him off "My Angel has already made arrangements with me over that your debt is clear you best thank her for that. Give her the half you have and from now on any and all deals go through Claire. Now who has been fucking over my clients? I will deal with him you deal with yours"

Lucius and Rage both look at me as if I've lost my damn mind, OK maybe I was being overly generous but they will need to pay me back so I'm not being generous just keeping the peace between the MC and my family. Lucius clears his throat and says " Mr Miller we don't actually know who fucked us all over. We only found out the other day and until we find out who our hands are tied on finding out who fucked you over. We have prospects currently being questioned but I have a feeling its higher than them. When we know I will tell Claire here and she can tell you."

"No Claire will deal with both problems that's what I have asked her for. She is family and I trust her to do what needs to be done. She will find both pieces of shit and you both can eradicate our problems. You and Claire hash out the details and she will inform me. I have business to attend to at the moment. Angel I will email you and please remember the previous email. Give the kids a kiss and cuddle from me and tell them I will call them tomorrow love you Angel. Goodbye Lucius and Rage enjoy your night" with that Uncle Graham hangs up. I look over to Lucius and Rage and heave a giant sigh. Both are looking at me with anger in their eyes. What the hell did I do? Why am I the one who always gets these looks ? I didn't say a damn word but oh no I'm the one who gets the backlash!

Gritting his teeth Rage asks "Why the fuck would he put you in charge ? Just who the fuck are you to him? "

CHAPTER 6

"I'm an enforcer for the family. I did have 10 years out but things need done on the quiet I do it Uncle Graham wants messy he sends the other enforcer. I'm angelic hence the name Angel. OK that's not really true he has called me that since I was born but I'm quiet. Did you originally think I threw that blade? Did you even think little ol me could do such a thing? No one ever does. And I'm in charge because the way you are doing this is going to cause problems in you club. What do you think is going to happen when you question so many people and they are bruised and bloody?" Lifting my eyebrow at them I continue "Questions are gonna be asked and you will need to explain what's going on which will ruin everything and you won't find shit! So here is what we are going to do. I will be in the club and we are going to set them up. That way we find out who and then why. OK ? Good. Now I have to sort shit for tomorrow I have someone to see and a traitor to my family to deal with and that takes talking to the other enforcer which I can't do with you here. Rage can we talk before you go ? I will be in the kitchen."

"Wait what do you mean you will be in the club? In what way ? Little girl this is my club I say what happens in it and when ! If I allow you in my club you do as I say when I fucking say it do I make myself crystal clear" Lucius states with a firm grip on my arm. Shrugging him off I turn to him, he's frozen when I do as I'm currently holding a 5 inch serrated blade to his cock.

"Tut tut Lucius. Didn't you get taught not to piss off a woman ? Don't ever touch me without permission again or this will be gone. Now to answer your questions I will either work the bar or just hang around although being Rage's Old Lady I guess I have a right to be there. What we will do is have a family thing and see who is watching what's happening. This may be your club but and listen when I tell you this. Don't for one fucking minute think I will take your shit. I will find these traitor's then you can deal with them. I ain't no little girl ain't been for a long fucking time you best watch how you speak to me." Walking away I hear him say "Fuck brother you better tame that bitch or she will have your balls in a jar "

I walk into the kitchen and go get a bottle of ice cold water from the fridge when I hear the kitchen door shut. A few seconds later I feel arms come around me. His arms feel so good around me feeling him put his hands on my belly. His hands on our child makes me smile until I remember he lied and made me think he was someone else I can't forgive that. No matter how rugged and rough he is he lied. Although I wouldn't mind another ride with him he is so commanding and that for me ohhh it makes my panties soaked. "Why? Why would you lie to me? Was this just a joke to you all in and out of jail something to pass the time ? If it is just turn around and walk away no harm no foul. I won't deny you your child but I also won't pressurize you into being there. That is your decision."

Hearing him take a deep breath and feeling him sigh through my hair he says "Claire Bear the only things I lied about was my name and my place in the club and that was because I'm a fucking idiot. No one had a laugh about it and they wont. And there's harm and foul to me I ain't walking out on you and our kids. I told you that your my Old Lady and you damn well better get used to it cause you ain't going no where.

Spinning me around he lifts me and I wrap my legs around his waist his hands are on my ass kneading the firm globes. I can't help roll my hips and grind my pussy against his thick hard cock feeling it pulsate against me. Groaning he sits me on the counter rips my top in two and growls "Fuck Claire your gorgeous! Tell me you forgive me. Tell me you want my cock in that tight fucking pussy again! Tell me now! " Biting on my right tit he slowly licks the bud and slides his tongue across my chest to do the same on my left. I arch my back feeling myself getting wetter grabbing his shirt I tear it in two I need to feel his skin against mine just as I'm about to lick his nipple he grabs my trousers and banks them down and off. Wow he is a master at that shit feeling my soaking wet panties being ripped off me all of a sudden I hear him groan "Fuck you're soaked this is all mine and only mine say it Claire I need to hear you say you're mine"

I can't think let alone speak I'm so turned on so needing to be fucked I automatically come out with "Rage I'm yours always and forever fuck me make me yours please I need you I need you so fucking bad it hurts" he plunges his tongue into my hot wet and wanton pussy "Fuck Rage deeper, lick my pussy, give me what I need" He slowly licks up my pussy to my clit and bites hard making me scream he slams his hand over my mouth. Unbuckling his belt he says "I'm fucking you hard I'm claiming you Claire your back will wear my cutt and when our baby is born you will wear my ink." Slamming into me I bite his hand and scream "RAGE fuck" grunting he pulls out slamming back in.

"Fuck me your so fucking tight I'm going to blow" hearing smashing plates and all I can think about is how fucking amazing this is feeling every inch of him hit that special spot every fucking thrust I'm so close to exploding he tilts my hips and I go off like a fucking bomb all I can see is sparks in front of me my whole body is spasming from the force of my orgasm .Rage slams into me one last time grunting "Fuck Claire I may need an hour to go again. You were made for me. Forgive me?"

Giggling "Yeah I forgive you but you need to do that again but try the bed next time and I won't have a spoon digging into my shoulder babe"

Getting up I head to the toilet next to the kitchen with Rage following me to clean up. He slaps my ass and says "I'm staying here babe any calls I want in on from now on. " stunned I just stare at him

"Try that again!? Any calls I make are private. You ain't privvy to my family and I ain't privvy to yours back the fuck off Rage this is something we need to get used to. "

I can see his jaw working "Behave Claire we will discuss this shit in the morning before I go back to the clubhouse." Shaking my head I clean myself then head to get the phone and computer. I need to speak to my Uncle check when Marcs flight arrives and do some digging into our family traitor.

Dialling Uncle Graham I check my emails he's sent a list of family who are here.

There's 4 makes it easier I guess. "Hello Angel did you get the list?"

Sighing I say " Aye I did, What time is Marc arriving? Why send him? Am I not good enough anymore or something? You know we can't stand each other so why answer me that question Uncle Graham! " silence for a good minute.

"Angel I need you to know I didn't want to send him. He demanded he go what am I supposed to do. Are you scared he is going to say something you don't like ? Simple plant him on his arse. Then work together like you used to well actually no not like you used to that's a bad fucking idea. He arrives at 10 am Tuesday meet him at the airport he has a flat set up in town already just in case this takes awhile. I'm going to go Angel I have meetings to go to. Oh just so you know I've sent your baby to you eta I will find out for you. Love you Angel "

"Love you too Uncle Graham" hanging up I take a deep breath knowing that Rage has heard every word I don't turn around I just tiredly say "I can't be bothered arguing can we do it tomorrow please I am so tired its unbelievable Rage. Stay or don't if you stay come to bed if not post the keys through the door." Heading out the room I head to the stairs. Climbing up the stairs I turn right and go in my room change into my pajamas and slide into my sheets just as I'm about to drift off I feel Rage slide in behind me wrapping his arms around me I hear him whisper "We will talk about this tomorrow Claire Bear" I nod then just as I'm falling asleep I hear "Daddy loves you little one"

CHAPTER 7

RAGE

Wakening up in Claire's bed alone is not the way I want to wake up but the smell of breakfast has me smiling. Stretching I get up and turn to the door and stop. Peter is standing in the doorway staring at me. "Morning little man. What's up?" He stares at me as if I'm a puzzle he can't work out yet. "I'm not little. And I want to know why you are in my mummy's bed. And why you are here." He has this look on his face that makes me laugh. "Peter isn't it? Well me and your mummy are together. She is my Old Lady, and I'm here because she and you and your sister are here. Got a question for ya though fancy helping me with a project today? Involves a bike I have at mine and I want to fix it up. Fancy it?" I've never seen a face light up so quick in all my life. Seems I've won the boy over. One down two to go! "Oh my god yes please are you really going to let me help? This is so awesome I'm going to go get old clothes on ". Running out the room and to his I chuckle. That kid is pretty cool.

Heading to the kitchen I hear " Mum why is Rage actually here? Makes no sense why he is here." Hearing Claire take a deep breath she replies " Ava he is my old man he is the man I was talking to and he is the father of your baby brother or sister. I know its going to be a massive adjustment but please for me try and at least be civil towards him and get to know him. Now there is going to be a family thing at the clubhouse and we have to go and I need to talk to you alone in a bit its about your real dad. I told you that Peters dad and yours are not the same and that your dad refused to believe me when I told him I was pregnant with you. Baby girl your dad is the other enforcer in the family and he will be here tomorrow to help sort the problem we have. Its up to you if you tell him he is your dad or if you want me to. Or if you just don't want to tell him anything this is a big decision but I have told you everything I have never held anything back. This is all on you baby girl. "

"No, he doesn't deserve to know me. You tried I was told by Auntie Lisa that she even tried and she still has the messages. I've seen them, he doesn't deserve me after what I saw. And wait does that mean I get to go to a party.? I need a new dress like now please mum please please please!!!! I will clean my room and the living room for a week promise!" Wow that's a surprise. To hear Ava sound so adamant that she wants nothing to do with her father is making my blood boil. How much of an asshole is this guy. But now I know my in with Ava. Let the games begin I will have my Old Lady and kids by my side.

Walking in the kitchen just as Claire is about to reply. I walk straight to her slide my hands around her waist and kiss her on the head "Morning gorgeous. How are you this morning? And did I hear you ladies talking about dresses?" Feeling Claire shifting her ass against my semi hard cock makes me want to slam into her hard but having to behave until later is going to be hard pardon the pun.

"Morning babe I'm good and hell no I ain't talking dresses, Ava is. I have maybe 4 dresses to my name. Diva over here has a wardrobe full so doesn't need anything new." Claire says with a smirk on her face and I just know she ain't gonna like what I'm about to do. "Hey Ava how about I send my cousin over who owns a dress shop with a few things for you to try on five dresses of your choice you can pick I will pay?"

Seeing her head shoot up like a shot and scream which nearly burst my ears. "Oh my god really??? You would do that ?! Mum please can I ?? " looking at Claire I can see she is pissed, but doesn't want to ruin the happy bouncing girl's mood after her hearing her piece of shit dad is on the way."As long as they ain't expensive and you will be doing work for Rage to pay for at least two dresses I will pay for two and Rage can treat you to one final offer take it or leave it young lady. And as for you Rage we will be speaking about this later but thank you"

Giving me a little kiss on my lips I can't help but grab her and take the kiss further. "Ewww that's something I do not need to see " hearing that I broke away from Claire and just stared at her. Seeing her blush just makes me want to take her here and now as I'm hard as a fucking rock!

Clearing my throat I say to Ava "OK kiddo I will phone my cousin after breakfast and babe I'm bringing a bike here for me and Peter to fix up so don't be mad but he needs to learn if he is around the boys from the club and they are all learning so not a word I want to bond with the boy please as well as you Ava I want us to be a family and it going to happen" watching my Old Lady smile so big makes me feel like a fucking god right now and as I look at Ava she is looking like she knows her mum is happy which seems to make her happy. Looks like both my girls just needed a bit of sugar and sweet to get them to my side good to know.

CLAIRE

I seriously just turn to a puddle of goo after what Rage just said. I swear these hormones are turning me into a sissy. But come on who wouldn't melt at what he just said who knew he was such a soft hearted man. OK he is probably sucking up mine and the kids asses but hey he will learn soon enough we will only allow so much suck ass til we get pissed off with it and we still need to talk about what's going to happen at the club this weekend. He ain't gonna like what I have planned and I don't care these little fuckheads ain't fucking with my family and getting away with it. "Hey babe we need a chat after breakfast remember and I need to phone my Uncle on an eta on Marc. I also need to check in with my work as I have this week off. I need us on the same page here" he looks at me like I've lost my mind "The kids know what's going on don't worry there and you need to know the code to the panic rooms just in case you need them" I'm gonna put some tunes on so I can start sorting shit out and putting some Dj Kurt on is a must The Power step is the first track and I bloody love it and so do the kids so I've got it turned right up while I sort the plan for Saturday.

ANGEL

CHAPTER 8

CLAIRE

Tuesday afternoon

Waiting at the airport for Marc to come off the plane I'm standing with Rage and he doesn't look happy at having to be here, but, I did tell him he didn't need to come to which he replied with a growled "Fuck no I ain't having him near ya, you're my Old Lady and he needs to know to fuck off asap babe." Kind of made me wet. OK totally made me wet but I digress. Just as I turn to tell him he can wait in the car I catch a sight of Marc and he ain't changed a bit which means he's still going to be a complete asshole. Oh well lets get this shit done. Knowing he ain't gonna like this plan but do I give a shit eh no I don't .

"Well if it ain't Angel in the fucking flesh still a bitch I see or have you learned your place."

Having to grab Rage before he kills him. I have a right good look at this wanker! He's dressed in a grey suit with a black shirt and grey tie. He has a black pair of shoes on, nothing really distinct about this prick, but hey ho his eyes alight on me and take me in. I'm wearing a pair of denim shorts that are fraid and a red cut off top which says Hardcore over it in white letters and a pair of black knee high boots with a five inch heel. Hair up in a ponytail and no make up.

Raising my eyebrow I state nicely "Still a bitch and proud to be, asshole. And how are you? Still a male slut?" Turning around I start walking to the car getting in the passenger side knowing Rage won't let me drive him anywhere, he gets in the driver side grabs me around the neck and kisses me his tongue slides over my lips asking for a full kiss and letting him the kiss isn't a soft one its all consuming and it makes me want to fuck him here in the car right now but he pulls away snarling "Mine". I couldn't help what I said I can't even say I didn't mean it cos I do it just is right feels right " I love you Rage" he freezes and then shakes his head as if to clear it turn the ignition on and drives away. What the hell? And in the back seat I hear a snort. Yeah he better shut his goddamn mouth or he will fucking regret it. What was that with Rage not a damn word and he has refused to even glance at me. Well fuck him he dares to claim I'm his yet three simple fucking words render his ass silent fine with me.

"Still can't keep a man I see" is snidely said from behind me. I can't believe he thinks for one fucking minute that he can talk to me like this and I actually stupidly said to Uncle Graham I would be nice. Breath Claire breath. He won't be here long. Looking out the window as I watch the trees and fields speed away I get my mind back on track.

I need to keep my head in the game its just another job. "So asshole why exactly are you here ? I can't fathom why you wanted to be here so why? What was so important that it warranted you to come and no fucking bullshit either." I ask calmly I ain't calm inside tho.

"I'm here to see this through, as I know your a bit rusty since you ain't done jackshit in ten fucking years bitch. Ten goddamn years since I last saw you and you insisted on telling me a lie. I don't trust you to pull this off, so I'm here to make sure you don't mess up. Pretty much like I always did." He slams his hands on the back of my seat to prove that point how he thought that was proving any sort of point I don't know. "OK" I can't be arsed to listen to his bullshit.

After dropping Marc off at the hotel. Rage and I went back to my house where he proceeded to say he had shit to do at the clubhouse and without another word or even a kiss he gets on his bike and peels out like there's a fire on his ass. Guess saying those three little words freaked him out. Walking in to the house Ava asks "Mum what's for dinner? Are you working tomorrow?"

"Hey princess yeah I'm working from 11 til 6 why what's up? And for dinner is Chinese I can't be bothered to cook. Fancy sitting in on the phone call to your great Uncle? If so shout your brother down too."

Ava looks at me and says "Yeah mum OK will just get Peter the now then we can chill with a film tonight just us" Guess my baby girl can see I'm having a shit day really need to get a grip of myself. I go to the living room and load up my email and there's one from Marc

From Marc

Subject work

Listen we need to talk we can't keep being like this Claire we need to work together as soon as this is done I'm going home. Phone me and we can meet at your house or wherever you want just not the clubhouse. I am sorry for being an ass but seeing you hit me hard all I could think was she ain't fucking changed a bit. I will be nice from now on. Phone me asap please

What? Just what the hell was that email this ain't the Marc I know he's a giant moron he ain't ever said he's in the wrong. So I do what he asks and phone him.

"Hey Marc I'm working from 11 so be at mine from half 9 as the kids will be at the sitters"

"Hey Angel that's fine with me. I am sorry for earlier being on a plane that long isn't good for my mood. You still tattooing? If so do you think you can squeeze me in while I'm here just gimmie a price. And you got any sort of idea who could have fucked us over?"

I pull the phone away from my ear and look at it like its in a different planet "OK this is too scary for me stop being nice it ain't you! Look come here at half 9 and we can discuss it all and yeah I have a space tomorrow at 1 til 3 email me what you want and I will give you a price, but stop being weird please your an asshole so be an asshole."

He is laughing at the other end and says "OK Angel no more scaring you. Will see you tomorrow going to scope this place out not the clubhouse that will be done via you and my watchful eyes at a later date. Enjoy the rest of your day bitch see ya the morn" he hangs up and just as I'm sorting what the hell just happened there he emails me a picture of Ava from when she was a baby.

To Marc

Subject tattoo

Can't do that. Portrait ain't my thing, I'm not comfortable doin them sorry.

Fuck him he ain't having my girl who he denied was his on his skin. Just as Ava and Peter walk in I hear a ping from my laptop. And as usual Ava looks over my shoulder to read

To Claire

Subject daughter

I want to see my daughter. I have the right to know her and you didn't try real hard did ye? I want a tattoo to have her with me at all times. You will allow me access as I'm already discussing with your Uncle that I want to move here. And he is starting to see reason.

Ava makes a low growl and snatches the computer from me and replys with

To Marc

Subject this is Ava

Here pal I want nothing to do with you I have seen the emails and you ain't ever been or ever will be my dad I ain't your daughter. Don't bother moving here I want fuk all to do with you you slimeball. GO AWAY!!!!!!!!!!!!!!!!!

I turn to her and cuddle her but also tell her off for swearing it ain't allowed by my kids ever. "So let's phone Uncle Graham then." I phone him and he answers straight away

"You just had to piss him off didn't you? Claire what the hell? Wait a minute... Ha no way did my Great Neice tell her dad to fuck off? She's so much like you Angel a bit too much"

Trying hard not to laugh I reply "Hey I did nothing but pick his ass up he was the one who started his shit. And yes she did what are you doin backing him moving here for I ain't liking that Uncle

Graham I seriously cant believe you would do that!"

Heaving a giant breath he states firmly " I ain't backing him I said its his life and that yeah he has a right to know who his daughter is but only if she allowed it which obviously she ain't"

"No I ain't. I, I don't want to know him he ain't my dad he wasn't there when I was born and he has never been there for me so why should I let him near me. I saw the emails and I don't like him not after that. Oh hi great Uncle Graham! Me and Peter are here." Ava says with some firmness but slightly trembling voice as if she's sure she will be told off for interrupting a conversation.

"Hi Princess and Prince how are you both? And Ava I totally understand where you are coming from. He was an idiot who didn't believe a word your mum and aunt said. I did tell him your mummy wasn't a liar but he was upset. Maybe try and give him a chance? For me?" He says. If I know my daughter she is gonna say no. Surprisingly she says "OK once and only for you even though I don't know you."

I'm sitting stunned. What just happened? I'm in the twilight zone or something, today is totally fucked up! Uncle Graham hangs up saying he will speak to me in a few days.

After dinner and a hot bath in a claw foot tub which is amazing and relaxing. I head down to get a drink and hear the double beep of the alarm that is my front door being opened without the key. Grabbing the pocket knife in my nightcoat, I text Ava and Peter to lock their rooms and stay in their cupboards until I say otherwise. Heading to the kitchen door I peek out and see a cutt I don't recognise. All lights are off downstairs and I hear 3 men talking quietly "This is gonna be easy go in grab her and the kids get out OK boys!" "Yeah boss" "No probs Sarge" Now ain't this fucking perfect ! Now they have pissed me off! Coming into my house thinking they can take me and my kids, swear people see a woman and kids and think well this is a good way to have people do as they ask eh no not in my house. Sliding through the door I make my way to the stairs and quickly run up them. Knowing I have maybe 2 minutes to get the kids safe. I unlock Ava's room grab her from the closet and run to Peter's room get Peter and get to my room without a sound. I open my cupboard and press the back and it opens my panic room I put the kids in it and tell them I will be back.

As soon as the door locks I hear "Shit the kids ain't here!" Wow these guys are crap at this. Grabbing my bag with my gun and blades I take a 3inch needle blade that I usually wear in my hair and 4 throwing knifes. Overkill yeah but I want these guys to leave not die scare tactic is a must right now. As they enter my bedroom I crouch beside my bed and toss the throwing knife at the first guy and it hits his right arm and his gun hits the floor I throw another 2 at the other guys just as the first starts crying out.

I then stand and say "What the fuck are you doing in my house? I would advise you leave now before you end up seriously hurt, they were just scratches!"

"Bitch your dead! We are the Silver Dog MC and you will die by my fucking hand. But I'm going to rip you apart first." The SAA snarled at me then the idiot beside him pulls his gun and I throw a blade between his eyes and he falls down dead.

I pull my gun and point it at the SAA and state "Leave now or you will die your choice"

"I will be fucking back bitch watch your back" as he leaves with the other guy I track them through the house.

After they leave I phone Marc who says he is coming over now. And then I phone Rage who doesn't answer so I phone Lucius "Who the fuck are the Silver Dogs and why would they dare to come to my house and try and take me and the kids?"

"Shit! Look we need to bring you and the kids in here at the clubhouse asap. Your not safe." Listening in I hear "Rage get that whore out Claire and the kids need help" I take a sharp breath and snarl "Fuck him he can keep his whore I will be there in an hour, I know the fucking way I'm bringing my other enforcer so get 2 rooms ready, and get your table sober. I want fucking words. My kids were in danger and your MC knew nothing ? Bullshit! I need the fucking goddamn truth and I will get it even if I need to spill blood Lucius. I ain't joking here." I hang up and tell the kids to pack a bag and get back to my room asap!

RAGE

"Fuck Prez ! Now Claire is going to think I cheated on her ass!!"

Trying to phone Claire to let her know I didn't fucking cheat on her. She's not answering and I know I'm going to have some hell to go through when she arrives. As soon as I can corner her she is being told this whore was in the back room giving the brothers a show not for fucking me I don't want her skank ass.

CHAPTER 9

CLAIRE

Marc arrives takes stock of me and the kids and wraps us in his arms "Fuck! Are you all alright ? I'm gonna do some looking into these fuckers. Where are you going" looking at Marc I say "We are fine nothing I can't handle but we need to do a clean up. You watch the kids while I deal with the twat upstairs. Ava this is your dad, keep you and Peter in his sight at all times"

After dealing with the dead man I come back in and tell everyone to get in the car and we go to the clubhouse. We walk straight through with everyone staring at us, mainly me as I have blood all over me. I slam into the meeting room not giving a shit, these fuckers put my kids in danger I'm way beyond angry. Pointing to Lucius I growl out "Who the fuck thought it was OK to not inform me that my family was in danger? And I want fucking names NOW! No one fucks with my family and fucking lives! Get my kids to a secure room cos this shit is being sorted now !" Lucius looks like I've pissed him off well now this fucker knows I ain't happy. "Claire back the fuck off or you won't like what will happen"

"Is that a fucking threat? Are you seriously thinking that I'm gonna allow you to threaten me, Lucius sorry pal but if this ain't dealt with you and I will part in bad taste. Get my kids settled in a secure room and we will sort this. I want this full table sober and here its time we sort this out so much for doin it nicely that just flew out the window. This is Marc the other enforcer for my family we will deal with who needs dealt with swiftly don't doubt it we are thorough and god help these fucktards who think they can mess with me and my family."

Lucius heaves a deep breath and counters "OK Claire table will be here. Just let me talk to them first before you start and we will give you the info on these guys. We will be involved ever step of the way. I refuse to fuck up what we have with your family. This agreement between us is working. You and I will talk privately later." Having that said makes me wonder what is actually going on that he needs to talk to me privately.

Marc takes the kids to a room at the back of the compound after I tell them to lock the door and do not open unless its me or Marc . I'm standing in a corner waiting for the room to fill staring at everyone walking in. Seeing Rage walk in I want to rip him apart he doesn't even look at me. And that is a bloody good thing as he's a waste of my time.

"Now brothers I want everyone to listen to what I say and I don't want to hear a word from anyone. There's a traitor in this MC and I want to give them the opportunity to come clean if not then Claire here will take over and it will be infront of me. So any takers. A shit load of money missing and the fact that someone dared to fuck with their own club is down right fucking disrespectful. I want a fucking name now!"

Seeing 2 people shifting in their seats. I lock on and walk over to them and slap their shoulders and whisper "Got anything to say boys? Even if its you have a feeling let me know as I can tell you ain't that fucking stupid." Teeth looks at me and whispers "Three seats from the Pres on the left ask him where he was a fortnight ago then last night after the Pres and Rage left. Now make it look like you know me and I ain't said shit." Standing up I kiss his head and say the kids wanted to see him while we were here as they liked having him in the house. Marc walks in nods to me and walks next to me kisses my cheek and breathes "Got some Intel you need to see, check your phone and damn you look fucking stunning in those trousers, fuck me Claire I've missed your ass. " huffing I say "Fuck off dickhead are the kids secure?"

 Grinding against me he says out loud "Aye all secure. Claire your Uncle wants a word and says next time don't drive looking like you came from a murder scene" laughing I say "Ha I will try, but that fucker threatened my kids"

Lucius slams his hand down on the table and roars "WHO FUCKED THIS CLUB OVER ? Claire your turn see if you can make the fucker talk! Everyone will stay in this room."

I walk to the guy that Teeth said and grab him flip him face down facing Lucius and shout "Where were you a fortnight ago? If you tell me this will go quick! If not my blade will sing with your blood" He stutters "Fuck you whore! Pres this bitch doesn't know shit I would never do you like that!"

"Brother this ain't on me now, she is the one out of pocket, it was her kids in danger I'm just here to watch what she can do. "

Slamming a serrated 5 and a half inch knife into his hand I take a step back hearing this asshole scream like a bitch is music to my ears. I look over to Marc and tilt my head asking if he wants in at this. He nods and walks over taking his rings off. He hates getting blood on them. He steps up behind me and runs his fingers over my shoulders and says "Angel I've fucking missed working with you, you ain't changed a bit, time for me to open this mans mouth. How about you sit on the table and watch how a man takes care of business. This fucker annoyed me. And I want him breathing for a while. "

Now Marc isn't being an asshole, he knows I won't torture for long where as he can keep a man alive for days which is pretty sick but oh well. I sit on the table right in front of the guy who is named Tag. Taking my phone out I see a message from Marc read it and slide it over to Lucius who reads it and looks pissed. On the text is a picture of Tag meeting with the Pres of the Silver Dogs.

In an hour Tag is singing like a budgie "The money I took and the Pres of the other club will kill you all and I'm going to laugh as he does it."

My turn I love this part. "Now now no need to be like this I'm sure we can come to some sort of arrangement how about you tell me what you want for the info you have on when the other mc will be coming to us?" I'm flipping my favorite blade it's a 4 inch flat blade with a fish tail on the bottom. And Bladez written in thick bold red letters along the side of the blade. This is my pride and joy and Tag is about to die by this blade.

"Let Sassy go right now and I will tell you what you want to know" looking over at Lucius with an eyebrow raised but before I can say a damn thing Demon roars

"What does my fucking Old Lady have to do with this you piece of shit!" Hearing Tag laughing "We've been fucking for 2 years she has been helping me feed the Dogs info on y'all." Before I can do a damn thing Demon grabs his gun and puts a bullet in Tags head well shit I needed more info. I start clapping "Well done idiot I wasn't finished."

"Someone get Sassy. I want her here to face the music." Lucius orders the men at the door.

RAGE

Well this day just went to hell, found out who our traitor or traitors are and Claire looks like a grim reaper from heaven but she won't look anywhere near me which is pissing me off as much as that Marc fucker putting his hands on my woman!

"Claire we need words and that fucker needs to stop touching my Old Lady"

ANGEL

CHAPTER 10

MARC

Hearing this fucker dare tell Claire I need to stop touching her makes me laugh. And what the fuck makes him think she's is his Old Lady. That ain't going to happen. I'm here now time to take back what's mine and this prick ain't getting near her again. "Where were you when her and the kids were in danger?"

"None of your business now if you can fuck off we can deal with this shit!" He thinks I'm actually going to leave. No chance so I just lean against the wall and smirk.

Claire let's loose and starts shouting "What the fuck is your problem? You dare to fuck some random chick and think I'm actually going to talk to you! Really? Don't see that one happening pal. Marc can you calm down and stop being an ass !? Thanks! Back to business Lucius what do you want to do? Do you want someone in their MC to talk or do you want someone placed in? And what happens with Sassy ?"

"I never fucked her, she was shaking her ass for the brothers."

Well didn't that just take the wind out my sails.

At that Sassy walks in hands on her hips "You wanted me Pres? "

"No I wanted you. Any idea why Sassy? You should know who I am !" Claire asks like sugar wouldn't melt. I know from experience when Claire stands with her feet tapping hands at her side but twitching at the ready to kick some serious ass. I've fucking missed this with her she makes me fucking harder than a stone. Fuck I was an idiot, who actually lets someone like Claire go? Me that's who like a moron and I don't have an actual reason other than I'm a fucking 6 foot 2 full of muscles fucking moron. I will get her back. That I fucking promise myself I will get her back.

RAGE

Hell no he ain't thinking he will just step back in with my Old Lady! She is carrying my goddamn kid ! Time to sort this shit before Mr I fucking had her first, decides he's going to try and have her again. Just hope she knows I'm telling the truth.

CLAIRE

Standing close to this Sassy bitch seeing her smirking as if she is lady muck. She is wearing a red see through top that comes to just below her tits and a pair of the tiniest blue shorts I have ever seen you can see the woman's knickers that's just disgusting she is making me want to slap the skank out of her and teach her to dress unlike a whore.

"Sorry who are you? And why would you want me?"

Really? That's the game she wants to play that's fine. Walking the length of the Oak table that has so many deep gouge's from being used for years. I run my fingers along it as I walk I can feel every indent. " OK Sassy. My name is Claire and I'm with your VP and I would love to know. Why the fuck you would talk to another MC? Surely you knew that someone was gonna be caught? Or are you that much of a fucking moron that your brain was telling your ass you were safe because who you were with. Which I can safely say that your both over especially by the look on his face he wants to leave and never see your skanky ass again. Women like you give us a bad name" I said. Yes OK I know that I will be telling Marc that he better fuck right off. I do believe Rage and we will talk and hopefully sort this shit out. I can forgive him being a fucking twat but he will be told don't fuck with me again.

"I didn't do a damn thing bitch! I certainly wouldn't sleep with another MC. And my old man would never leave me so you can go fuck yourself. Coming into my clubhouse and trying to run it. Having your little shithead kids be here and making us uncomfortable. "

She's cut off by Lucius and Rage both roaring "Your fucking clubhouse??" (Lucius) "Watch who your fucking calling shithead kids bitch" (Rage)

Seeing Demon slowly realise what she just said he grates out "No one said anything about sleeping with another MC. So not only have you fucked over this MC, my fucking family, you've been spreading your legs for others? Bitch I'm done take my cutt off now!" I have never seen a man look so hurt in all my life. As much as I despise Demon I feel kinda sorry for him. Well time for me to leave I am just going to take my ass to the room my kids are in and settle for the night the men can deal with this shit on their own.

"Well I'm going to check my kids and get food I'm hungry and need sleep. I'm pretty sure you lot can deal with this shit! Rage you and I will talk tomorrow. Lucius you need me come get me but if need be just keep her locked up and I will deal with it tomorrow but I do need my kids to stay here where I know they will be safer until I sort the house."

Rage stares at me as if he's about to lose his shit "Claire give me an hour I need to talk to you tonight we will secure this bitch and I will meet you at my room the kids are in the room next to mine."

Lucius just nods while looking like he is about to do some serious damage to someone, which I seriously understand. "I will phone your Uncle for a word, but you and the kids will be here throughout lockdown. I will get the prospects to pick up some stuff if you give me a list of what you need"

I just nod my head at both of them I'm too hungry and tired to deal with an argument.

"Where am I sleeping ? Same room as Claire?" Marc pipes up with a smirk.

"Fuck no you ain't. She's in my bed she's my fucking Old Lady you piece of shit" Rage growls out with a look of pure rage aimed straight at Marc.

I look this twat up and down and say "Are you seriously that stupid? Did you think that I would just open my arms and my legs just cos your here? Really? Hell fucking no! Marc back off. Me and Rage are together simple as that. They will find you a place to stay and you can see Ava tomorrow" with that I head off to check the kids.

Seeing they are both fast asleep I give my babies a kiss and leave to find the kitchen.

CHAPTER 11

CLAIRE

Walking to the kitchen I hear "Who is this skank ? Does she think coming here after our men is going to happen? Fuck no I had Rage today and I plan on being his Old Lady soon. I've paid my dues its about time I was made an Old Lady. "

"Yeah Lou-ann she has no chance he will be your ol man soon she don't have shit on us. She looks like a fat bitch anyway. And how gross was she when she came in covered in blood. That's just disgusting !"

At that I walk in blood and all and seriously I don't give a shit what these bitches think. "So you are trying to say you slept with my man? Very much doubt that, he wouldn't touch you're skanky ass when he has me! And as for the blood, sorry not sorry my kids are a hell of a lot more important than thinking I have some sick fucks blood on me. Unless you can mouth off to my face do me a favor and fuck off thanks muchly" with that I grab a bag of crisps\chips and head back to the room my kids are in no way in hell am I going near his room after that shit.

RAGE

Sitting at this table thinking about everything that has happened in the last hour. I look over at Demon and see he is devastated about what has went down and I don't blame him. That whore fucked not only him but this club over. I really need to see Claire and sort this shit out between us out. What a clusterfuck and a half. Although my Old Lady is fucking gorgeous when she's in action.

"Well brothers this is just a fucked up situation, we will stand by Demon on what he wants done to Sassy, she is his Old Lady so he has the right to make the decision when it comes to her. We will make a plan of attack for the devils bitches and we will be on lockdown immediately get everyone here now. I will say Sassy can stew in the cell for a day or two and we will deal with whatever then. Now Claire and the kids will be here and I'm assuming this Marc guy will be here as well although that isn't confirmed we will assume he is and get used to him being here. Brothers I've got to say I never thought we would be fucked over by not only one but two of our own. And to have outsiders be the ones to find them as well as attempt to deal with them,well I'm ashamed. This should have been dealt with by us not them. I'm in much need of a beer and some pussy, but, sadly I need to find Claire and talk to her and make sure her and the kids are OK. Demon come see me in about an hour and we will talk."

"Pres go get a drink we will have a meeting tomorrow and discuss what's our next step" I say but all I want to do is go to Claire and the kids. I need to sort this but my brother comes first. "Demon come get a drink and get drunk I think we both need it" Getting up I put my hand on his shoulder and squeeze. We both leave the room and go to the bar.

A whore sways her skank ass over to me and rubs against me and squawks in my ear "Hey baby fancy taking me back to our room and fucking me like you should then let me show my ol man how much I care for him" I can't help the laugh that comes from me "Bitch you ain't my Old Lady so fuck off. Go find another brother. My Old Lady is currently in my room waiting for me I don't want or need you near me so why don't you stop spreading your shit and get gone."

"Oh and tramp don't come between Rage and Claire again. Trust me you don't want Claire taking a strip out your ass. Actually that's something I would love to see so keep it up." Demon grunts at her. Her face is fixed in a scowl. Why the hell did I go near her and wreck what I was starting to have with Claire. Oh fuck this, its time I took control instead of acting like a fucking bitch Claire will just need to learn I'm the man and what I say goes.

Turning to Demon clink glasses and say "Bro how you holding up?"

Heaving a sigh he looks at me and says with dejection "Rage brother I have no fucking clue. But I do know we need to kill the bitch and I don't think I can do it. But she needs gone after we get info from her"

I agree with him and I know I couldn't but he is right "Why don't we ask Claire what she thinks as she still needs to find her traitor" just as I say this Claire comes into the room with what looks like nothing but my goddamn Harley T-shirt. Well that shit won't fly with me. "Claire what the fuck are you doing?! You can't just walk your ass in here looking like that! Get your ass back in my room NOW!"

CLAIRE

Is this idiot for fucking real? I walk my ass out the shower to come face to face with a whore on his bed naked and he thinks that I'm going to be nice fuck no! "Oh darling, thought you would like to explain why a whore is on our bed naked. See I was going to drag her ass out and show her who's man you were, but then I thought, surely he ain't that fucking thick that he said yeah just you get in my bed and I will be in shortly, no surely not. Why don't you deal with that problem while I see if Marc is available for a meeting. We will be in the corner. I love you hun try not to fucking run and freak this time please. Get that skanky cow out my bed and change the sheets please."

Fuckin idiot seriously some men have no fucking idea! After sitting in the room with the kids for 10 minutes I decided to stay in Rage's room. Yeah when I walked out and seen her laid on my bed spread eagled I swear I could see right through her pussy she was that wide. That alone will give me nightmares. And when she said Rage told her to be waiting I knew she was lying I can't stand a liar.

CHAPTER 12

RAGE

FML! Really not only do I have shit to deal with, with Demon, I now need to march my ass down to my room and kick this whore out. And I know I'm going to get agro from Claire for this, just once I would love a laid back day. Walking down the corridor Prez walks out of Trisha's room with a satisfied look on his face. Smirking "Hey Prez" Lookin at me as if he knows I'm going to get some naughty sex he says "Hey VP going to see your Old Lady? Tell her I say hi"

"Sadly Prez no I'm about to throw some skank ass out my room"

"This shit I need to see! Who is it? And why is she in your room? The club girls know not to come to our rooms without us."

Heaving a deep breath and releasing it I grunt out " Lou-ann. And she, as far as I know, told Claire that I told her to be in my bed waiting. Claire walked out and this idiot is naked on my bed spouting shit to Claire. She needs to learn her place Prez I ain't having this shit come between Claire and I, we have enough shit to deal with."

Shaking his head "Well let's sort this shit out shall we"

Stepping up to my room we hear drawers being shut, we push open the door slowly and see her putting something in my underwear drawer then watch as she puts something in Claire's jacket pocket. What the hell ? Looking over at Prez he mouths what the fuck?! Yeah that's exactly what I want to know! We both back off from the door and quickly head back to the bar. Passing a few brothers we motion for them to come with us to the corner Claire is in with Marc. Seeing him near her makes my blood boil. And I know there's nothing going on, still makes me wonder why they look so cosy, but, this is a little more important. We need Claire and Marc to know what's just went on as well as our brothers. "Yo Sexy quick question. Did Lou-ann say anything strange to ya"

Looking at me in question she smirks saying

"What other than she was told by you to get naked in our bed? No why? What's happened now? Can I please have one day where I can chill out, no drama, nothing, please. Is that really too much to ask for? I really don't think it is."

Well shit ! "After this baby we will go away for a week just me, you and the kids. How's that sound ?" She has a big smile as she replys "Yes please!"

Just as I go to tell her and my brothers what's happening now. I hear. "Claire, sadly, being around these guys you will never know what peace is." Just as I'm about to strangle the live out this fuckhead, Prez says "What the fuck did you just say? You actually thought I'd allow you to speak like you know us in my own damn club? Yeah you can fuck off before I put a bullet in your goddamn head, boy! Go back to your hotel and stay there until we either need you or you hear from your boss, asshole!"

Seeing his face turn red and expecting him to make it worse, which I would love just to see this guy get his ass handed to him he grates out "the only one to send me away right now is Claire so pipe down pal". His eyes are spitting hate towards my Pres and I ain't having this shit. "Shut up idiot, you are in...." " Marc get a grip go back to the hotel I need you to pick up a few things and bring them tomorrow please. I need a break from all this agro and arguing just one night of peace please.". Claire cuts me off. He still refuses to move. "SYCO!!!!" I don't even need to search as he has been at the table next to us. "Yeah VP what's up?"

 "Escort this guy to his hotel and get your ass back here, take another two riders with you.". Syco grabs him and says " Yeah VP" seeing the look Marc gives not only me but Claire sets me on edge. Definitely keeping and eye or two on him.

Turning to Claire I say "Somethin just happened baby and I need to know if there was anything weird, other than her being on our bed, that she said or did."

"Nope not a thing babe, Why? What's happened now ? I was serious when I said I wanted one night of peace. Tomorrow night you, me the kids and maybe Demon if he gives me a smile, can watch movies and chill. Please Rage, just one night, one bloody night is all I ask! We will sort this next problem and then have a drink and head to bed, we need to talk and I mean a serious conversation.". She is looking at me, with I swear her heart in her eyes.

She is turning me into a soft bastard. " OK babe one night off and us to talk tonight. But after we talk your ass is mine. Both Lucius and my self walked to our room to see that whore, right when we get there we hear drawers being opened and see her putting something in my drawer and then for her to put something in your jacket. We need to know if she said something or seemed off in any way." Looking at her I see her mull over what I say and she says " Not really all she said was you sent her there.".

Time to find out "Babe can you go back to our room. And make like you're getting ready for bed.

We will listen to what she says if she says anything. Don't make it seem like you know what's going on. I will come in with Demon and we will cause an argument to get you out the room. We will take it from there.". I say with some malice behind my voice. I'm sick of my Old Lady getting in to shit. This is my club time the members started taking it back to the way it was. I've already spoke to the Pres on this and he agrees, we have got fucking lazy.

CLAIRE

OK this I need to see. Personally I would just go off on one and haul her out, but this is not my house, so not my job. I've got enough to sort out, like my house and find the snake in my family. Although he can't be of my family as they would all rather die than turn on family. Right now though I get up and calmly lean over, and give my man a kiss then leave the table heading back to the room. I sneak a peek and see this slag is still on my bed. Seriously? Time to move bitch. Just as I walk through the door my phone ping's. Ignoring it I look at her and see she has a smug look on her face. Inwardly rolling my eyes "You may want to move I don't want the smell or feel of slut on my body.".

She sneers at me and says "Well that's not what my man was saying earlier so get out my room interloper"

Laughing (come on I can't help it) "Here idiot ye might want to try that again. My man not yours. Now fuck off and sleep somewhere else" Just as I say that the door bangs open and both Rage and Demon slur some words about stupid bitches and pregnant asses. And stagger into the room banging off a wardrobe.

"Lou-Lou just the whore I need! Step this way and suck my cock!" Rage points at her.

"What? Are you fucking serious right now? And what about me and your fucking child?". OK I know this is all fake but what the actual? Bit of warning would have been nice.

"Aw look Rage its the one who isn't sure who her baby daddy is. Who do you think ? Me? You? Or that Scottish fucker? Will we toss a coin? You dodged a fucking bullet there brother. She's worse than these whores here, and that's fucking saying something since they don't wear much clothes and take at least 3 brother's in a day!" Demon better watch his goddamn mouth, before I introduce my foot to it.

Huffing I shout "Fuck the two of you! I'm gone after tonight I'm leaving this town and you best hope I never come back. Fuckin enjoy ya skanky whore!" I storm out taking my bag and jacket but not before I see her look at my bag and smile. Yeah idiot I'm going hunting. Leaving the guys to it, I make my way to the bar to speak to Lucius and see if I can get a room to look in this bag and jacket. "Lucius can we go for a quiet chat just somewhere private." He looks up from his glass nods and steps up. He looks like the world is on his shoulders. Poor guy has had a hell of a day.

 Fuck it deal with this, then check the kids and go to sleep. We walk to where the guys hold their meetings, we pass a few guys coming and going from rooms. Walking in the room I put my bag on the table and methodically check it and eventually find what looks like a small button. Now I use these little fuckers and they are really cool when I use them not so much when they are used on me. Ohhh I'm going to have fun taking this tracker on a little trip in the next couple of days. Test the car time yay!

" I need your permission to come and go for the next week Pres. I'm going to bring the owner of this little toy to us but I need my Uncle here or even my cousins here to take the kids as they ain't gonna be around for this shit. No chance. "

"Set it up. But put the call on speaker"

Pulling my phone out I call my Uncle Graham "Hi Angel, what's up? Everything sorted? Marc called and said he.." Cutting him off I say "Yeah everything could be better. Need a favour can you come over? If not you send my cousins over I need them to watch the kids for about a week. Til I sort a few things. I'm important well important enough to warrant a tracker, and its active. When is my car here? "

"About a day away Angel. And of course your important your my Angel! Both me and the guys will be over I need to bring Stacy with me I need a favour but that's not massively important right now I will book tickets and head over. Keep eyes and ears open Angel. Take care of those babies til I get there" hanging up I turn and say "Well that was easier than I thought"

CHAPTER 13

After sitting in the room with the kids for an hour, I give up thinking Rage is coming to get me. So I fall asleep. I wake the next morning with the kids asking for food, since they don't have a clue where to go. We go searching the kitchen for food and Lou-Ann comes in looking like the cat who got the cream. This bitch better not say a damn word. "Mum, what we doin today?" Peter asks. "Wee man right now I ain't sure. I've got to check my emails to see if we can go to the airport now or later" Ava shouts "What why?? Where are we going? Are we going away because of what happened at our house?" Looking at Ava I can't help but feel like shit. I'm sending them with my Uncle to get away from here. I would rather I had eyes on them but knowing my Uncle is taking them well away and that they will be safe is the only thing keeping me steady.

"Princess we are going on a holiday and this is something we will discuss in private. I think it will do us good to get away from what happened, too much has happened and we need a timeout and a reset our emotions. As well as certain people we need to get away from." Raising an eyebrow silently telling Ava and Peter something is amiss and to keep it quiet. She nods and states "Well I want to go to Disneyland." Shaking my head with a smile on my face, I finish making French toast.

"Thank god for that." Is heard behind me. Stilling and barely holding my temper and tongue. I pull out my phone after feeling it vibrate in my pocket. I see a message from my Uncle saying that he is just getting on the plane and that was sent at 2am. What made my phone vibrate is an email from Marc.

From: Marc

Claire, I know we always agreed our signals for me to go. And it was a good thing I left. I can't Talk Through Email as I have a Bad signal. And the phone is A Shit kind. So meet me at the house in a bit. Oh I saw a teDdy at the mAll aNd Needed to get it for ava You should have seen the poor lassie at the till. I will see you in a bit

Well then seems phone and emails are hacked and no doubt by Danny our hackers son. Would never have thought it was him. Well shit! Now what the hell am I going to do? I'm now going to have to tell Uncle Graham that one of his longest friends son is working against us. Swear my life is like a fucking film!

UNCLE GRAHAM

What a horribly long flight. All I want is a beer and my bed. Sadly I'm not getting that. I have to book myself, Stacy, Johnny and Craig into this hotel. Wait on Angel appearing with the kids whom I've never met (which pisses me off) then hand off Stacy with Angel, which is going to piss her off, but, hopefully she understands and helps us out. My Stacy was adopted and her junkie mother and father think its OK to try and involve my competition to get my baby girl back. Good luck to them finding her here, never mind the fact my Neice will happily slaughter those two with a smile on her face and a skip in her step. She will hit the goddamn roof when she appears. Been a long ass time since I have seen her never mind wound her up. I've even got a week and a half, maybe more with my great Neice and nephew I'm going to show them how to wind her up. Its a right of passage for Angel and she needs to go through this. I'm so glad I'm on the other side of the world.

Chapping at the car door signals me that we have arrived at our hotel.

Getting out the car I turn to my little Princess "OK Princess your cousin should be here. She is going to take care of you and keep you safe. Please don't loose sight of why you are here, keep safe and close to Angel. I will deal with the shit back home, then you can come home. I wish I didn't have to do this but I need you safe, and Angel can and will do that. She will show you the ropes with weapons so you can protect yourself. Please Princess don't hate me for this. I hate myself enough for the both of us"

Stacy looks at me with her heart in her eyes, that's the thing about the women in this family, they open their eyes and shining bright is their hearts. Tears you apart every bloody time. "Daddy I know why this needs to be done but, I want you to stay. I'm scared for you with everything that's happening. You are my daddy not that piece of shit. Why did they have to come back ? I could never hate you! I will do as Angel says, but I also want to learn how to tattoo. Do you think that would be OK to ask her to teach me?"

My Princess has never met Angel and vice versa but I know these two will get on there's 8 years between them, I adopted Princess seven years ago. She gives me hope as I'm showing her that people do love her, my men would kill for her in a minute. I will be when I get home, hence why she is here. I don't want her around when it all goes down. Hearing Princess inhale sharply I turn and see my Angel, god she looks just as angelic as she did when she was a baby. She is part of what's amazing in my life. Her parents were good until they died. "Angel!" I shout. She turns and runs into my arms. She is shaking and to be truthful so am I. Damn I've missed my Neice. "Hi Angel, you gonna introduce me to my great Neice and Nephew? I need you to meet my daughter Stacy, I call her Princess."

"Oh my god! Daughter? How did I not know? Hi Princess I'm Claire. This is my daughter Ava and my son Peter. Kids this is Uncle Graham and Stacy who is your cousin." Smiling from ear to ear she hasn't changed a damn bit!

"Let's head up to my room and get the kids settled. I need a word Angel." We trapse up to the room getting settled and I ask Johnny and Craig to take the kids to get food and ice cream. Knowing I need privacy and silence for this chat.

"Angel what I'm gonna say is going tae piss ye aff, and I need ye tae hawd yer tongue just for a bit. I need ye tae take Princess with ye for about 6 months, maybe more. Her junkie biological parents have got some heavy backing to try and get her back. It ain't happening no way, she is my wee girl. The heavy backing is Wully's family. And I ain't having her being round this shit. I need you to help her come out her shell, I've maybe been a bit selfish wae her and not let her out my sight she's never been on a date, never went to college. Never experienced life. She wants to learn to be a tattooist. But I need you to teach her weapons, I'm not always going to be there." Looking at her, she's shocked, well that's a bit o an understatement. Her jaw has dropped to the floor and for once the little shit is speechless. I need a picture of this shit. If anyone knows my Angel, they know she's outspoken and certainly doesn't shut up.

"Uncle Graham I will watch her like she is my own. But why is she coming with me the now? Wouldn't it be better tae take her with you and the kids? And I've got my own little bomb to drop, Danny is the guy who stole from us. I can't use my email or my phone. I've been followed here by another MC, and some skanky bitch has bugged my bag and jacket. I'm going to take the fuckers tracking me on a little trip after here though. Is this really the way to bring Princess into the fold?" She's hitting her lip nervously. She is worried and I don't understand why. She has never been like this I am calling her on this bullshit. My Angel is fucking strong, she has never been nervous or skittish. "Why are you nervous?"

"Its been a while since I have had to not only defend myself but others Uncle Graham. The other night I was scared shitless. I had to kill a man in front of my kids. I had to show my kids a side of me that will no doubt haunt their dreams for years to come. And now you are asking me to protect Stacy. Do you understand how much this unnerves me? That you are placing her in my care and trusting me not to fuck this up?" Seeing her nervously twisting her hands makes me laugh.

"Angel you're a force to be reckoned with, people back home still fear you. And I have so much faith you will protect my Princess I don't trust her care in many but you, Johnny, Craig and Tony. Marc scares her. And I understand why. But you will, no doubt in my mind, will care and watch her like one of your own. Now when you say Danny, you don't mean Brian's boy do ye? Surely he ain't stupid enough to fuck over his own family? I'm going tae phone Brian and see if he knows anything about where his boy is as he is supposed to be in Glasgow." Pulling out my phone I pull up Brian's number and press call.

 "Hey Brian any idea where Danny is?........ Hmm you sure? As my Angel has just said he's here in the States. Have a check please as I've just been informed he has been a naughty boy and fucked us over for half a mill..... What do you want done? Bring him home for an ass kicking or treat him like a turncoat? ... OK ... That bad? Why didn't you tell me he was using? Why didn't you let us deal with the first load of thefts? ..... That wasn't your responsibility Brian I would have just left it as an understanding between us. How much has been taken ? .... And you put that back by your own hand? We need a beer and a chat when I get home later. Angel will take care of it. Do you want the body home or left.? Uh huh OK brother. I will phone you later."

Hanging up I turn to Angel "To dust Angel he has stole around £600,000 never mind the half a mill. I want him gone in a puff of air. His own father is fed up of being a scapegoat".

Looking up into her eyes I see rage in them. Been a while since I've seen this look. Damn shame I won't be there to see her at work. She is bloodthirsty when she gets like this. She nods and says " OK next problem then. Marc. He needs to realise that I'm not on the market, get him to back off. He can see Ava and help with this shit but I have a man and I don't shag about never have never will. I'm also pregnant so its a definite no." Nodding at her I affirm I will have a word.

Chapping at the door alerts us the kids are back and our conversation is ended but not before I fling her the keys to the car that's parked in the parking lot. She smiles big knowing her baby is just outside.

Kids come running in the room barely missing the blue and white floral vase "Kids slow down, we are not a bunch of animals" I say and at that its like breaks on a car they come to a screeching halt.

"Uncle Graham, the big bald guy in the black T-shirt says we are going to Florida , is that true? Do we get to go to Disneyland? Do we? Mum please say we do?! Please?" Peter looks like he is about to explode with excitement.

Looking at the kids I smile and say "Yes we are Peter. We leave in 12 hours, so you will stay with the big bald guy, who is Johnny, and Craig who is the one with the white T-shirt and brown hair. Your mum is going to take Stacy with her and once we get back she is going to be staying with you for a while. I need you both to help her settle in and show her the ropes around here. Can you both do that for me?" Big smiles and nods come from the kids then its a free for all in the screaming department. God I love my family.

"Princess I need you to know that Angel will take care of you. Now are you sure you don't want to come with us? I need you safe and I know either way you choose you will be as Angel will watch you like a hawk, but you will be in a clubhouse with a bunch of bikers. " she looks up and looks straight at Angel and says "Daddy I will be fine. She is my cousin and I trust my family. Plus not only will she teach me weapons I also, no offence, don't want to go to Disneyland. I can't do screaming excited kids." We all laugh at that well except the kids, they are still jumping about.

Getting off the bed I grab my Princess in a bear hug. I wish I could keep her with me, but I need her safe. I'm going to deal with this shit back home, these fuckers will be in their graves within a month. That I promise myself. And there's no doubt in my mind I will have blood on my own hands and I can't fucking wait. No one fucks with my family and lives. "OK girls time to go. I don't want a hard goodbye as I will be here for another 3 weeks after we get back from a wee holiday with my Neice and nephew. But I want this problem dealt with in the time I'm away. Angel I have Tony meeting you at the clubhouse. The MC know he is coming. He is there for whatever you need."

STACY

Knowing that I'm staying here because of the sperm donor and the human incubator just pisses me off. I'm going to be away from my dad for as long as it takes plus some. I hate this. But upside I get to meet and get to know Angel. I have heard so much about her that I actually feel like she should be my sister not my cousin. Looking at Craig I really am going to miss him. I've had a crush on him since I was 15, but he has never been interested. I have seen him with so many different women that he has kinda made me realise Craig isn't the one for me. Maybe me being away really is a good thing. Get my head clear.

CLAIRE

Nodding to Uncle Graham. I turn to the kids and make them promise to behave, the kids have never been away from me. I'm gonna miss them so much but being away from this shitstorm will keep me focused on the job and not on the mind blowing worry if they were around this shit. Giving them both tight cuddles, I turn to Johnny and take a long look at him. He's standing at 6ft muscles popping from his neck to his feet I swear he is just a tank. He is covered in tattoos and has a few piercings. He obviously shaves his head but looks like a slight psycho, bet he is a giant teddy bear though. Craig looks more like a steroid head if I'm honest. But the look in his brown eyes makes me know my kids will be safe. That's all I need to know. Heading towards my Uncle I say "Take care of my babies Uncle Graham. I will take care of yours. Come on Princess time to get back"

CHAPTER 14

CLAIRE

Knowing that as soon as I leave here, I'm going to be followed makes me shiver in both anticipation and dread. I have Princess with me and I ain't too sure how she is with speed in a car. "Hey Princess, what ye like in a car ? Are you OK with fast driving? Cos we are going tae have some idiots up our ass. I need to know you ain't gonna freak out huni. If you are please let me know now." Looking at her she looks fine, but looks can be deceiving.

"I'm fine with it. Craig usually drives fast, around 100 mph. And that doesn't freak me out." She looks down at her feet. OK shy doesn't work for me, I'm going to have to pull her out her shell. How the hell is she like this when she has been brought up with my Uncle Graham. Saying that she was with her own parents and I don't have a clue what happened there, not my business unless I'm informed.

"Princess I will be going faster. We will no doubt be out running motorbikes. Fuck it! We will see how you get on. Come on and we will go get my baby."

Talk about excitement, yeah that's my baby she is a Subaru Impreza 2.0 she is sky blue with gold alloys. She is a speed machine. Can't believe Uncle Graham has kept her this long and she looks so pretty! Registration plate reads ANG3L. I've had this plate since I was 17. Her name is Suzy Subaru

Sliding into the car I put the key in the ignition and turn. Suzy purrs like a fucking tiger! "Hello baby, I've missed you." Turning the stereo on and slide some Dj Kurt in. First track is MDMA. Love this track, all I can do is laugh at poor Princess's face she looks like I've lost my mind. Turning out of the car park under the hotel. I phone Rage. "Hey babe, just leaving the hotel. Will be home in about an hour. Remember what I said earlier. As soon as I phone you open the gates. I'm scared of being out

here without you. Wish you had came with me."
Let's hope whoever is listening actually believes
the damsel in distress act. I actually want to be sick,
hearing this shit coming out my mouth. Knowing
I'm strapped with not only my 9mm but 46 knifes
and there is, or should be, 25 blades in this car.
Let's hope these little fuckwads come after me.

"Babe you will be fine I know you are scared and
worried but I told you, you have nothing to worry
about your ol man is here and the gate will be
sorted. Now get your ass home. I want food."
Hanging up I say to Princess "Ready Princess? This
is going to be fast, but first wave to the nice men
on the motorcycles. Those are the ones who you
will see scramble to follow this car. Then they will
follow me all the way to the clubhouse and I will
explain the rest as we get closer. Ain't jinxing this.
Now if you could go into my bag and grab the
remote looking thing, I will introduce you to a little
thing I call payback from a bitch." She pulls out the
remote link for a little tracker I put on 4 bikes
earlier. Shows they don't think twice about
allowing a big titted woman to not only touch

them but their precious bikes. Now Rage won't allow anyone near his bike. The kids ain't allowed near his bike ffs. "Press the little green button please Princess. Don't look so worried, its just a tracker or 4 honestly, look at my phone as you do it you will see 4 dots on the screen. I need you to monitor those dots. This is massively important. If any of them rear off or go too close I need you to tell me. We are the centre dot at all times everything else.."

"I know what this is. Dad shown me what this does and how to work it." She has a smile a mile wide. Damn she may have just been shy, but like me, give her a job and she will, so far, step up to the plate. "Ok then, window down, track change and wave Princess. We are about to have 4 pretty pissed off bikers on our ass." Winking at her I change the track from. Powerstomp is here to Dj Kurt - I'll fucking show you messy. Tooting my horn to get these men's attention. Princess and I wave with smiles on our faces. Come on boys follow. Putting my foot on the accelerator, I quickly change through my gears and quickly hit 80mph through the back streets of the town. Heading towards the interstate, I put my foot down dropping from 4th gear to 3rd and Suzy fly's. Damn I've missed this car. "How we doing over there Princess? How's the dots?"

"Dots are good about half a mile away from us and closing. And this is actually fun. Please say you will teach me how to drive like this. Dad won't let me drive ever. Something about you and Marc escorting him to a meeting and women never allowed to drive him again. He wouldn't elaborate other than to say he doesn't want to experience that shit again. What did you do?? Dots are a quarter mile away."

Omg really, he is still bitchin about that !!! "I will tell you over a beer or ten. Haha honestly yes I will teach you how to do this. Just don't tell him I taught you, he will never give you a car if you do. Right up ahead we will be taking a hard left and going down a dirt road.. SHIT!! OK new plan wing it! Keep an eye on those 4 dots those are important." Up ahead about 10 bikes are roaring down the road towards me, well shit time to play dodgems.

They will move putting my foot down further we reach 130mph. Been a long time since I've fucking done this. Thank fuck these bikes move out my way. They may be idiots but they are idiots who don't want to be splattered over the asphalt, and they were driving the wrong way. See fucking idiots. Gritting my teeth I phone Rage "Need another route hit a snag. Couldn't take the turn. "

"OK Babe, you will be coming up to another turn, take it. Then I want you to head to the clubhouse. Its the way you would have went to your house anyway. Get here as soon as possible you are about 15 minutes out. See you soon. "

OK new route sorted. Time to haul ass. And bring these fuckers some pain. "Angel 2 of these dots are nearly on our ass. The other 2 isn't far behind. What's the plan? God I never thought I'd hear myself say that! " OK 2 directly behind, now I know where I am I know these roads. Smiling I say "OK Stacy now I teach you how to watch my butt and my side mirrors. Slide your seat back 3 clicks. I need you to watch both side mirrors. And let me know if you see anyone directly behind as I'm about to slam on the anchors. When fuckwit one and two come down the side. "

"ERM both sides? Cos that's wits happening. No one behind at the ... Shit! Warning would be nice!" She screams that last bit as I slam my brakes on and turn into a side road. Foot back on the gas I gun it knowing I have maybe half a minute to get some distance. Heading past the farm at the bottom of my road I make a sharp turn right and know I've got maybe 5 minutes to the clubhouse. I need these guys close so I ask "Where are the dots? "

"Nearly on us. We have 5 bikes behind us but not seriously close."

OK Princess this next bit is a you stay in this car its been reinforced. So STAY HERE. I promise you will be safe but I want you to lock these doors and not move. Promise me now you will do as I ask. I will be parking the car at the far end of the lot. "

"OK Angel. I promise but I want a beer after this shit." She huffs. Well tough shit toots what I say goes here now. Speeding up I am about 2 minutes out. "Angel one is falling back." Ha fucking got you. "Tap on the dot, and click trace. Let the fucker fall back. Where are the other 3? " she quickly replies "Directly behind us"

Speeding through the gates I go to the far end of the building and turn to Princess "Stay here lock the car til I get back, do not allow anyone in this car. No one do you hear me. There's a snitch still in this clubhouse. I want you alone when I get back." Sliding out the car I pull out my gun and point it toward the gate that these fucker have just came through. The guys are currently surrounding them. I walk up to their VP and say "Did you want me for something? Or is this just a social call?"

"Fuck you bitch. We want our money. Danny said the way to get it is through you. Don't care if its on your back or not." He spits at me.

Raising an eyebrow. I turn to Lucius "Any chance I can gag this fucker?" Turning back to the VP I say "So any idea where your Sargent at Arms is? Seems he bailed pretty quick when he realised where we were going, may I also add, you are a royal fuck up. Surely you should know where this clubhouse is ? Any of you lot should have known. And you though you could take me and my kids and scare them ? Fuck no! Take them where ever you want to. I have an arsehole to find!" I head to the car when I feel Rage behind me

"You OK? Did the kids get away OK?" Rage asks. He has his arms around me from behind. It feels so good to be in his arms, I didn't get a cuddle or a kiss this morning before I left, even knowing this plan.

 Ah well. "Yeah I'm fine, or I will be when we finish this. Kids are fine, but my cousin is in the car." We head off toward the car he turns me and kisses me deep. I grab him by his T-shirt and lick his lips to gain entry to his mouth. Jumping up I wrap my legs around his waist and cling on. I need him inside me I need him so bad.

CHAPTER 15

CLAIRE

Shit! Stacy! Letting myself drop to the ground I turn to the car saying to Rage over my shoulder "I forgot Stacy. That's your fault, being a sexy fucker. Is this place still secure?"

Seeing a smirk on his face he replies "Yeah babe, all secure"

Opening the car I tell Stacy to come out. We get her suitcase from the car and make our way into the clubhouse. Seeing her eyes bulge out her head I try not to be seriously pissed off with my Uncle. How could he not acclimate her to our way of life. Yeah OK ours isn't quite like this with the bar and naked women, but come on.

Looking around I see Demon and Crank staring at us or more precise Stacy. Oh hell no! Crank is a manwhore and Demon is not using my baby cousin as a damn rebound. Not a chance. Looking at them with a scowl on my face they see me and Crank puts his head down, Demon just can't take his eyes off her. I will let her know later right now I'm needing chocolate and my bed.

DEMON

After dealing with the shit storm outside I came in for a drink. After being fucked over by my ex Old Lady, all I want is to drink this shit away. But club business needs doing, and no doubt Claire will want some help. Looking around I look for a club girl to fuck for the night and come to a grinding halt at seeing one fucking sexy bitch, she is slim but not too slim. I'd say she even has curves, blonde hair can't see her eyes but she looks so lost. Tits that give Claire a run for her money. Fuck what would it feel to slide my cock through then and fuck her tits til I shoot my load over her neck.

Sitting with a rock hard cock imagining her. Claire and the sexy little bitch come over "Hey Demon this is my cousin Stacy who is... Princess? What age are you ? Just thought I wasn't told."

Stacy or Princess ? She suits Princess better. She looks at the floor and replies to Claire "Angel I'm 20 turning 21. Daddy likes to let people think I'm just a kid"

Smirking into my bottle, all I can think is yeah I'm going to teach her some shit. Rage will kick my ass but fuck it.

CLAIRE

After settling Princess in, I head to the cellar to sort this shit out time to find Danny's ass. Walking through the door I hear skin hitting skin and smile. Adrenaline coursing through me all I can think is time to scare some men into spilling some secrets.

"Now is that anyway to treat guests?" Every man down here which includes Rage, Demon, Crank, Leo, Lucius and Tony all look at me like I've lost my damn mind. And to a few it would seem that way, but seriously, Tony looking at me like that? Really? Has he forgotten what I'm like?

"Surely you offered these men a beverage! No? OK then Tony can you go get me a glass of ice water and a bucket of boiling water please?" At that he smiles wide and says "Damn Angel I've missed you! So fucking polite when your about to unleash some hell. God help these fuckers." He runs upstairs to get what I need.

"Now I'm going to be nice and ask one time only, then I'm going to show you how I got my other name. Where is my family member that is called Danny ? "

Looking straight at me he spits blood on the floor "Fuck you bitch. I'm not telling you shit." Of course he's not going to tell me turning my hand out of my pocket, I pull out a nail file and slice it across his face from under his right eye to his lip. Then begin to clean my nails with it. "Care to try that again? I'm not one to fuck about pal. I know just where to cut what to slice without you dying for hours even days. So will you answer my question or not? Ahhh Tony just in time. Care to take some of the salt in the corner and add it to the bucket. Thank you babe"

The fucktard in front of me tilts his head looking at me like I'm still not a threat. Strolling over to him I crouch down and stare straight at him and smile sweetly and slowly side the nail file into his thigh, not only feeling it pop his skin I hear it and he grits his teeth hard. Pushing it in to his leg all the way to the handle I repeat "Care to try that again?" And twist the handle, he grunts and says nothing. "OK then next up"

Going over to the table I roll out my blades. Looking for the 6inch long serrated blade dip it in the salt water and turn to face him. I skip the short distance and ask for someone to go through my music and turn it on. Dj Kurt-Passion pours through the speakers. Slamming the blade down quickly into his left hand I twist and pull it out slamming it into his right hand just below the middle knuckle I leave it there. And take the bottle of water and drink it. I empty it on the floor and put some of the salt water in it. I then pour the water over his hands and oh does he scream. "Your a fucking psycho bitch"

Hearing a soft laugh I turn to Tony "Tony do you happen to have that knife I gave you years ago? " he smirks and pulls it out his strap attached to his leg and hands it over. "Anything for you Angel" looking at it its a normal flat bladed knife except there's a button in the handle that releases an inch and a half spike from the handle so that when you do stab someone it latches on. Walking over to Demon I whisper in his ear "He fucked your ex Old Lady. Do you want a piece? If so stay clear of his heart and any area that will likely kill him quickly."

Demon takes the knife and asks "Do you have anything to say motherfucker?"

"Fuck you asshole." At that Demon stabs him in his gut.

"At this rate he ain't going to survive that long but I will get the info. Why don't you guys go upstairs and relax, Tony and I won't be long. If someone could take Princess something to eat that would be good."

2 hours later Tony and I come up to the bar. I hand Lucius a scrap of paper with info on who exactly

fucked the club over. And we know where Danny is. Tomorrow we will hopefully find and eradicate him as well as the other member of this club and the little whore who thinks she has one over on us. "Someone is on clean up duty. I need food and sleep. Has anyone checked on Princess?"

Rage looks up and stands taking me in a hug and whispers "We have it in hand baby. Go get something to eat and I will be in bed in a bit. Love you baby." My jaw drops, all I can think is oh my god, that voice saying love you.

RAGE

Seeing the shock on Angels face makes me smile. I never thought those words would come out my own mouth. But I meant them, she is my Old Lady, she's carrying my kid and she looks hot as fuck with a blade and a gun in her hand.

"Where is Demon?" I ask Crank

"Took Princess to her room but that was about 10 minutes ago, so fuck knows. He is either fucking her or has went for a long ass shower. Fuck I'm about to go for a cold shower after seeing that hot little bitch."

"Unless you want that tiny fucking cock of yours cut the fuck off brother, I'd advise you shut your mouth!" Demon growls at Crank.

"Fuck brother, where you been. And I was only joking no need to get fucking aggressive over her. Take your aggression out on her pussy not on me motherfucker" snarls Crank. Swear these two will always butt heads over stupid shit!

"Shut up the two of you now! Demon you know she is off limits, she's Angels cousin for fuck sake. Keep your dick out! Church in the morning brothers. This shit needs putting to bed, talking of bed I'm going to go fuck my Old Lady! "

DEMON

Half an hour ago

I can't keep my eyes off her! She is keeping her eyes downcast. Makes me wonder why she is here, no one has told me so I'm guessing it must be something serious enough for her to move across the world. She is sexy as fuck and she will be mine! I refuse to allow my ex fucking whore to make me fuck up the rest of my life. I've had my drinking binge now its time to have some special woman in my life. Now I just need to make sure Angel doesn't kill me first! That woman is fucking deadly!

Turning to Princess fully, I say gruffly " Princess do you know where your sleeping?" Yeah she will either be in my room on the second floor or the room right next to it.

She looks directly at me and says with what seems to be shyness "No Angel didn't tell me, just said to wait here"

Raising an eyebrow I say "Well I will show u where you will be staying during lockdown. Follow me." Getting up I head towards the stairs, turning around I see she is about 10 steps behind me so I grab her hand and pull her along when really all I want to do is pick her up and carry her caveman style. Taking her upstairs I take her to my room. I had one of the club sluts clean everything out so its clean and none of that bitches shit is here. I sit her on the bed. "Babe this is my room you can sleep here. Now I know you're here to be with your cousin but you are one sexy bitch and I want between your legs. I want you as my Old Lady. You are not to touch another man ever. I can't claim you yet I have a bunch of shit to work through but you will be mine best get used to it and quick!" I push her shocked but red faced body down flat on the bed and dip down to kiss her. She doesn't disappoint and kisses me back while mewling and rubbing her hot pussy against my hardening cock. Fuck ! This bitch is reving my engine hard. Pulling back I ask "Was the reason you left a man? Do I need to kill a fucking piece of shit who thinks your pussy is his?" She shakes her head hard and I smile.

CLAIRE

As I'm waiting for Rage to appear I start to snoop. Yes I know bad Claire, but I'm bored! Seeing a box I lift the lid and see all the letters I wrote him. Lifting one of the ones at the back I read.

Dear Demon

As I write this my kids are in bed I have a glass of beer and I'm reflecting on things you said a while ago. You need to explain exactly what an Old Lady entails. Is it that im your girlfriend? Wife? Does it also mean that if you cheat will I need to just live with it? I'm sorry actually no I'm not sorry I will never be the kind of woman who will sit and do as you say. I was brought up in a family who are strong willed. Who don't allow others to walk all over them as if they are shit on their shoe.

If you were ever to cheat on me I would never forgive you. I would walk away and you wouldn't see me for dust. I need you to understand when I'm with someone I'm with them no one else!

Change of topic. You have 4 months to go til you get out. What do you want to do the minute you get out. Well other than get on your bike and drive? You will need to send me your normal address for me to continue writing to you. Well that's if you ain't sick of me yet haha.

I found a new rave outfit. Can't wait for Ravers I need a good stomp. I'm currently listening to a set by Dj Kurt and Joey Riot. Yes I know I'm forever listening to Dj Kurt but he is in my top 3 artists so I can't help it. I really wish I could send you a CD but sadly I'm not allowed.

Well I'm going to say goodbye for now, as I'm up for the kids and work I've got a full schedule tomorrow. Love you.

Hugs and kisses

Claire xoxo

PS I've sent a new pic of me hope you like.

Well shit! I do believe he didn't cheat so I need to just put all the fears aside. I am carrying his baby.

Best put these back and just step away. Hearing my phone ping a message. I look on the table and spot it.

Tony: Incoming your man is on his way. We need a family meeting in the morning. Not majorly urgent just need your sizes for that thing we were talking about earlier. I found it for ya.

Me: Yay thank god ! Does it look pretty?

Tony: Oh yeah you will love it when it arrives.

Me: OK thank you Tony so glad you found it can't wait.

Now that's some good fucking news. My family are awesome at finding shit!

The door opens and Rage steps in. I can't help but admire the man. He is built like a tank all muscles and tattoos. I just want to lick him, swear I have drool on the side of my mouth which I try to slyly wipe just to make sure. He chuckles seeing that and runs his eyes all over me. Making me shiver and pray that he will strip me lick me and fuck me !

"We'll darlin don't you just look like a fucking sexy Old Lady. I'm going to have you tonight best get ready to be unable to leave our bed for a few days!"

Huffing out a laugh I say "Cocky much? Your cock is huge but it ain't made of that much staying power. Although I'm happy to see if you can go the distance."

Snarling at me like I'm a gazelle and he's the big lion. He comes over lifts me up. I grab his arm and feel all those muscles against my skin. Turning us so he is on the bed and I'm on top, he runs his hands down my arms around my waist then softly cups his hands around my belly and says "Now son I need you to go for a sleep for a few hours while I have my way with your mom. Love you my boy"

"Ehh how do you know its a boy and not a girl? We don't know. She may be a girl. And hey who says your getting lucky tonight. I may just have a headache. Pretty sure I can feel one coming on." With that I feel a slap against my left ass cheek and laugh.

"Angel sex is a cure all. Didn't you know that ? Now strip and let me slam my cock in you til you feel me for days!"

CHAPTER 16

RAGE

Knowing my kid is in her belly, I can't help but smile. This sexy little minx is all mine and I'm about to show her exactly how mine she is. I roll us so she is underneath me. She has my cock standing to attention instantly. I slowly strip her taking my time with her panties, starting at her neck I run my tongue down to her breasts and swirl my tongue round her nipple then softly bite, which makes her arch her back. My Old Lady is a fan of this shit! I am a tit man well tits ass anything really but she gets my motor running like a teenager. As I continue down her belly I get to her pussy and nibble her clit. Hearing the sharp intake of breath I smile then flatten my tongue to run up her pussy tasting what must be the fucking elixir of life. Feeling her start to rub her pussy harder against my face I know she must be about ready to explode and give me her cum. And cum she does.

She tastes of heaven. Hearing her scream my name is the icing on the fucking cake.

"Rage I need your cock! Now!!"

Just as I move to line my cock up to her pussy she flips me over onto my back and grins at me "Not that way yet babe"

She grips my cock in her hand and slowly runs her tongue from base to tip. Swirling her magic tongue around the tip. I have to grit my teeth to stop me from slamming my rock hard cock in her mouth. My woman knows what she is doing with her tongue ! Slowly she wraps her lips around my cock and slides down my shaft she hits the back of her throat with my dick and all I can do is grip her hair thanking everything that's fucking holy that she is my woman. Fuck she can deep throat without gagging! I'm a lucky fucking bastard!

She is bobbing her head up and down sucking my shaft and I feel like I'm about to blow down her throat. I quickly slide out of her mouth. She moans because of the loss of my cock. Gripping her by the arms I slide her up my body and kiss her hard.

Wrapping my arms round her, we roll so I'm on top and between her legs.

Looking down at her I see the biggest smile on her face. Well she's about to have a bigger one once my rock hard cock slams in her pussy hard.

"Ready Claire Bear?"

"Mmm yeah, I'm ready Rage. I need your cock in my pussy. I'm so wet. "

Lining up I start teasing her rubbing the head of my cock between her folds and she is soaked, slowly I sink my 10 and a half inch cock in to her hot, wet pussy. Closing my eyes due to how tight she is I feel like I'm going to bust a nut as soon as I'm fully seated. Claire starts squirming wanting me to stop teasing her well tough shit this is my time and I want her begging me to fuck her hard to make her scream my name so loud she has a sore throat and everyone knows who she fucking belongs to. ME, ONLY FUCKIN ME!

"Rage please, please fuck me. I need you please."

Just as she says please for the last time I slam home. She screams out "Fuck!!!" And I start pounding into her. Knowing I'm going to have to hold back for the sake of my kid in her belly. Gripping her hair and kissing and biting the side of her neck. She can't stop wriggling which makes me thrust faster and just as I'm feeling like I'm going to cum I slow down even though she is trying to use her heels to keep me going.

"Babe slow down. Its my turn so fucking behave or I will stop. You don't want me to stop babe. "

She quickly fucking stopped trying to top from the bottom. That shit don't happen. Ever. Gripping her hips I start to pull her up to my cock then think no time to fuck her from behind, so I slide out and flip her onto her knees. She flips her hair over her shoulder and looks at me with a smirk. "Fuck me hard Rage now!"

Fuckin happily! Time to make her scream. Sliding slowly back in her pussy she cries out and I know its because she is feeling every fucking inch of me slowly spreading her pussy apart to accommodate me. Fuckin love the feel of her. She's so goddamn tight. Its like a vice. As I start fucking her getting faster and faster. She is screaming my name over and over. Feeling my balls tighten I know I'm about to blow giving her one last hard thrust. We both cum at the same time. Tightening my grip on her hair I shout "Fuck Claire!" While she screams my name.

I roll off to the right side of her and tuck her into my side and just close my eyes trying to calm my racing heart. All I can hear is a mix of my heavy breathing and hers, as well as her doing an unbelievable little laugh. Like she can't imagine I'm that fucking good. Well she better believe it.

"Love you Claire. Once our little girl or boy is here I'm getting you inked. Go to sleep we will talk in the morning babe"

Just as I finish saying that I look down to see she has passed out. Chuckling to myself thinking I sound like a pussy bitch thank fuck she probably never heard me. After getting myself and Claire cleaned up I switched the lights off got in bed curled up with my Old Lady and promptly fell asleep.

CHAPTER 17

CLAIRE

1 Month Later

Walking out to my car seething mad, after being told we still can't find Danny or Moss. After a goddamn month. Surely they ain't skipped the bloody country. My kids are at school and I'm going for a drive I'm back at work tomorrow and if I see that fucker Jones again I'm going to kill the bastard. He has been up my cousins ass for weeks now and he's due a lesson on what stay the fuck away means. Seriously how many times do I have to say fuck off. Surely that's blatently to the point but oh no he still comes back for more. Best go a drive and calm down before I lose my grip on this temper. Rage has tried to calm me down. Sadly it didn't work although I'm pissed at him too. Not 5 minutes ago he came out with, "Babe you're acting like a fucking psycho chill will ya" What the actual fuck?? Really?? Yeah that's really going to calm me down! Men!

Getting into my car and speeding out of the clubhouse. Not looking anywhere but forward. I drive through the town not noticing there's a motorcycle and an SUV behind me. Hearing a beep from the console in my car I look down at it and smile. Gotcha bitch.

Behind me is the fucker we are looking for. Picking up my phone I call the Prez "Have you calmed down yet Sugar? Ready to come back ?"

Smiling "Well I would if my little tracker didn't show up right behind me prez. Mind doing a favor get Teeth to track me there's a tracker in my ring. Although I'm not getting out this car. I'm going a drive see how far he follows and go the back way to my house. Meet us there. If not place a few guys around the area in a 20 mile radius. Time to play."

"Watch your back we will buzz when we are set up! Take care of that baby. Granddaddy wants her safe."

Putting some DJ Kurt on cracking my neck I leave the town and put my foot down. Cat and mouse it is then. Feeling that rush run through my body when I put my foot down on the accelerator there really is nothing better. I would say its better than sex but well no just no I have Rage in my bed nightly. Hearing 666 Daze blaring through my speakers I start singing. Hitting 100mph on the straight road knowing I can go over it but playing with the fuckers behind me and plus there's no way the fucker in the SUV who I'm gathering and secretly hoping is Danny can keep up with the speeds I'm about to put them through. OK the bike can but im needing him to.

Dropping gears and speed to take a tight turn. I see the SUV has dropped back but this fucker is still on my ass. Good. He better stay there. My phone rings seeing its Princess I answer "Not a good time babe what's up ?"

"Guys have left said to tell you that if you give them 10 minutes they will be mostly in position. Demon says I had to stay here. I'm not happy but he asked to get the cages ready. So I'm doing that.

Have fun love ya biatch. Phone Demon or Rage if you get into some problems."

"See ya in a bit Princess. Can you pick the kids up from school please this may take a minute. I want this fucker on fumes. Shit!! Phone the guys don't care who, the SUV wants to play chicken"

Hanging up I put my foot down who the fuck in their right mind wants to play chicken ? Not fucking me but, hey, he may but I'm a better driver. Taught by the best. And no wankstain is going to best me. And especially in a bloody suv. Heading straight towards the moron at the last second he swerves right. Idiot! Hadn't even noticed I was leaning towards the left of him anyway! Seeing in my rear view he has stopped and beginning to turn around. The biker is still behind me I take the slip road to the back road towards my house. I shout for my phone to ring Rage he answers with a roared

"Where the fuck are you?"

"Fuck you to dickhead! I'm on the back road to our house. 15 to 20 minutes out be fucking ready! I want both the biker and the SUV driver in those cages today! No fucking mistakes please. And please have remembered we have that appointment tomorrow at noon. Love you baby"

"Claire I swear you're scatter brained at the minute. Ready when you are Angel. Bring them by for a chat and a beer why don't cha?!"

Hanging up I shout for the phone to call Lucius "Be ready. And for once baby is sleeping with the occasional kick. See told you settle the baby in the car but does anyone listen to why I go a drive at 3am nooooo of course not! 10 minutes out Pres. "

Hanging up without hearing what he has to say I press harder on the accelerator hitting 106mph on the straight knowing I will be in my back garden in less than 8 minutes and these fuckers will be held in the cage for my fun later. Well once I've made dinner and spent time with my kids of course. Mummy duties first its a must. Nothing comes between me and the kids. Biker boy is still up my ass. Why he insists on being there I don't know he must like giving it up the ass. I'm going somewhere just not without him. He's my date tonight as well as Danny boy. Hopefully finish this shit tonight. Would be a weight off my mind. I don't even care about the money now I just want to relax through the rest of this pregnancy and see if there's anything I can do to help out my Uncle back in Scotland.

Turning down the main stretch to my house. I can see the SUV backing off. Oh hell naw! Danny you ain't leaving this party yet! I'm about to do something monumentally stupid but that SUV will stay with me if I need to do something seriously drastic. I take my foot off the accelerator and start to slow to 45 mph making it look like something is wrong with the car and what do you know ? Can you see they actually fell for this shit. Total eye roll here. Just as the SUV comes to my side I see there's a truck coming down the road a Ford F-150 and that is one of my boys. Putting my foot back down shifting back through the gears I can literally see my back gate which I'm about to drive through. Can't be helped and I will fix it when I have time. Just as I go through it I turn the wheel making my car spin to a stop. And I see the biker barrel through the break in the fence, and my guys pull up around him on their bikes. Damn that's a fucking good sight to see.

"Hey Angel got fuckhead number 2 in the truck. He may have fallen asleep. But it looks a dead ringer for your Danny if I do say so myself." Crank says as he opens my door.

"All in a good drive to calm down. Damn such a busy day. OK move need to to check the car." I laugh.

Rage can be heard in the distance saying "Get their asses in the cage back at the clubhouse. I'm about to slap my Ol ladies ass for this shit. She pregnant and doing this shit. She is going to give me a damn heart attack with this shit!"

The guys all start laughing. I start to walk around the car to check it, Demon and Rage come to me and look at me as if I've grown 3 heads. Seeing a shitload of scratches I want to cry! My poor baby!! Oh someone is going to bleed more for this! OK I did it to my car but I digress this wouldn't have happened if it wasn't for those two making me crash through that fence and I cant exactly kick my own ass can I! No. So they can deal with an ass kicking to the ninth degree. Turning to the guys I pout and turn on the waterworks (come on needs must and all that. I want my car fixed). "My car! My poor baby is all scratched and dented. And the insurance ain't going to pay out for 'driving to capture morons' what am I going to do? This will cost a massive amount and there's no way I can do it on my own, I'm pregnant and can't do it. I'm going to have to sell it and then I will be without a car and then how am I going to get about. How am I going to take the kids to school and to the park and sports and school activities. How am I going to get the baby home from the hospital Rage? How?" (I totally used everything in the book and these guys are falling for it ha!)

Rage looks at me and wraps his arms around me in a bear hug and says "Angel we will take care of your car until then use my truck baby. Now calm down we will get you some ice cream that you like and you can relax until the kids are home and we will order in tonight, just let those fuckers sweat it out in the cages for tonight. Call your Uncle and let him know what's happened"

See told ya total sucker. Although Demon has a giant smirk on his face which may mean he saw me smile ahh fuck it! I'm getting my car fixed and I get to drive the big ass truck. Go team me! Kids will be happy.

"Thank you gorgeous. I'm just going to go in the house and pack a few things up for our stay at the clubhouse. Let me know what to order for dinner. Unless you want me to make something for the boys as well."

Walking up to the house I hear Demon say "Bro I don't know whether to slap you upside the head or get down on my hands and knees and praise Angel, your ass just got played like a fucking violin. She knows as well as I do that that car would cost around 3 grand to fix and that's including a full respray. Yet you not only told her you would get it fixed but gave her your truck. OK I know what I need to do. " Hearing a slap and Rage shouting

"Fucker when you get an Old Lady like Angel you do everything to keep her happy as well as her pussy open and willing to take your cock at anytime. Fuck if she asked for me to deal with this bullshit and let her rest I would jump at it, but, Angel won't let this slide. I knew those were fake fucking tears but she smiled after. When you find another Old Lady who is deserving the fucking title you will know what I'm talking about"

I walk into the house and don't hear he reply. Gathering all our clothes and a chocolate bar, I head outside seeing Rage standing against the truck smirking at me

"Babe you're a shitty actress but you can still have the keys when I ain't driving you around. Don't wreck my paint job."

My mouth works but no words come out. What the hell do I say to that? Nothing I just fling the bag at him and tell him I want two tubs of ice cream and grapes asap.

CHAPTER 18

PRINCESS

Standing at the bar washing glasses one of the club girls is standing in front of me staring at me she spits on the bar top and smears "Well if it ain't the Princess. No one around to fucking protect your ass now is there? No Angel no Demon no fucking body. You need to fuck off back to your own country. England must be missing its little miss prissy. No one wants you here. You don't fuck the brothers no one will touch you. Doesn't that show you that you're not wanted never mind you are fucking ugly and look like a fucking child. Angel only uses you as a babysitter for fuck sake. Just leave bitch!"

Sighing, I knew this was due. After Angel and Pres declaring me a Princess to the club to protect me, I've had these sluts, especially Candy, come up and spout similar crap. Its starting to get repetitive now. Can't they come up with something new. Like 'Hi how are you? Missing your dad?' Looking directly at her I smile and say "I'm from Scotland hen not England. Big difference in accent, please clue in tae that. I may be ugly but at least I don't need to get down on my knees for a little attention. I don't need to get tested every week either. Angel may not need me but I'm family. And sweetness, I certainly don't need the protection of the people in this club against you. What's the worst you could currently do to me right now? Hmm? Spit on me spout yer shite ? Oh I know give me an std!? Fuck off I'm not in the mood for this shit! Go back to opening your legs and stay clear of me."

"Fuckin cunt!" As she screams this she smashes the glass I just cleaned into my arm on the bar. Digging in the glass she takes a bit and swipes it across my face. The second she does that I grab her hair and slam her face first into the bar and nowhere near the glass. Just as she hits the floor I move out of the bar and head to my room to see what damage she has done and to grab my keys.

I'm gone! I'm not dealing with this crap anymore. I grab the cash I have, my phone and some clothes and lastly my keys to the car I bought a week ago. I go to my car and pull out the clubhouse, just as the brothers all start to arrive I've got my face covered with a soft scarf and a pair of sunglasses. I head to the hospital 2 towns over with tears in my eyes. My arm and face are hurting but I'm getting away from the madness that is that club. I can't handle it anymore. Mostly its everything to do with Demon. I can't watch him with another club whore I just can't. After everything was said he sleeps with all of them yet won't even look near me? No ! I'm done!

Sitting waiting to be seen at the hospital, I text Angel.

Me: Need to get away for a while. Turning off my phone. I'm fine just need a breather get away for a little holiday for a week. Sorry but I need space. You will need to pick the kids up from school. Glad you have got who you need. I will phone dad so he knows. Marc went back to Scotland to help dad today. Love you.

My name has been called and I'm being seen by the doctor.

"How did you come by these cuts?"

"I fell against a glass and it got my arm and as I turned my face I scraped it off the broken shard. I'm a klutz."

He fell for that. "Well we will need to stitch you up then you can leave no need for an overnight stay."

Thank fuck for that. My phone pings with a text

Angel: Wtf?? Kids are sorted Princess. What's going on ? The guys said Candy was knocked out at the bar and there's blood and a broken glass on the bar. And you left as they were coming in. Demon is going mad saying there's blood in your room and that your clothes are gone. What happened? I understand needing a breather but just stay at my house for a while don't leave.

Me: Too late Angel. When that bitch comes to ask her what happened. Tell Demon that Candy was right. And so was he! After all I heard what he said last week. I'm just a kid to everyone. Give the kids a cuddle for me please. I have money I have my car and some clothes I've been stitched up. I will now have a nice scar but hey can't make me any worse may even make me look badass. Will contact you as soon as I get somewhere to sleep for the night. Won't be on this phone will use a burner. Love you.

Just as I send that my phone pings again

 Demon: What the fuck? What did you do to Candy?

Me: Yeah fuck you!!! Bye asshole!

Angel: Stitched up? As in hospital? What did she fucking do?? What did Demon say ?

Me: Yes hospital but I'm OK promise. Permanent damage is what she did as well as gave me an awakening Angel. That life ain't for me. Speak in a bit.

Demon: What?? What do you fucking mean bye? Get your ass here now! Stop being a fucking brat

Demon: Actually fuck you ! Go back to your dad I'm done babysitting your fucking ass!! I was right you're just a child. You may have a tight pussy but I'm swimming in pussy! Bye bitch

And that right there is exactly what he said the other week to Crank. Phoning my dad I say

"Daddy I'm OK just going for a week or 2 holiday. Will use the back up card. I've got plenty in it. I will phone you or email you daily for your peace of mind. Wish I could just come home though."

Hearing him take a deep breath he replys "Princess you were safe with Angel. Why did you leave and no bullshit either. Tell me the truth."

I know he won't stop until I tell him but I also know he will send someone to kill her and him.

"I was my usual klutzy self dad. I cut my arm and face but honestly I'm good. I just need a holiday away from greasy bikers. I will email you when I get to the hotel. I'm going to drive now. Love you daddy"

"OK love you too Princess you better phone me when you stop though."

"I will daddy" hanging up. The doctor walks back in to do my stitches and sends me on my way with the instructions of how to keep it all clean. Getting back into my car I pull out of the hospital and just drive. I don't care where I go along as it's away from here. Away from him.

DEMON

Walking into the club after seeing my Princess drive out of the clubhouse. I stop dead in my tracks. Candy is on the floor in front of the bar, there's glass and blood on the bar. Someone had a fight. What the hell is going on now! One fucking day of no goddamned drama. Is that so fucking much to ask?

"Candy babe wake up. What happened?"

She came too looked at me for a minute then started crying. I hate bitches who cry!

"She attacked me Demon for no reason. All I asked for was a drink and she smashed a glass on her arm and sliced her face! She's a psycho! She slammed my head into the bar. Please tell me she's away from here. I'm so scared!" Knowing that I will check the camera feeds in a bit I will find out if that's the truth or not, but right now I'm needed downstairs. After heading downstairs and dealing with our new guests. I go for a beer then decide I may as well check and see if miss Princess is back she should be by now. As I approach her room I see blood smeared on the door handle walking in her room there's nothing here. What? Why? Fuckin bitch left!? Checking where I know she stores cash. There's none. She left ? Why? I told her we would make a go of things. She mustn't fucking care. See why I don't trust bitches. They have no hearts. I've got to find her to know what happened I don't fucking believe that whore. I send a text.

Me: What the fuck? What did you do to Candy?

Baby: Yeah fuck you!!! Bye asshole!!!

Me: What?? What do you fucking mean bye? Get your ass here now! Stop being a fucking brat

Me: Actually fuck you ! Go back to your dad I'm done babysitting your fucking ass!! I was right you're just a child. You may have a tight pussy but I'm swimming in pussy! Bye bitch

I don't know why I am so angry she wont fucking tell me what's wrong and if she is OK. But my life won't go on hold for her.

Angel comes storming in her room. Shouting "Don't dare tell me you believe that slut downstairs ! She is lying go check the tapes I know Princess ain't a klutz. And I swear if my Uncle phones me because of this your head will fucking come off asshole! Bring her back now!"

"No"

She stops dead and looks at me like I've become shit on her shoe. "What ?"

"I said no. She wants to go ? Fine she can go. I'm fed up of chasing her and watching her. I'm not her man I'm just an easy fuck, actually no she was an easy fuck. I'm done Angel no more. Now I'm going to check the feed and get the truth for everyone. But I just don't care anymore. Sorry."

I walk to the computer room and watch what happened. I decide Candy is gone. She fucking lied. She started this shit. She has caused the club Princess to leave and not be happy in her own home. But I'm not going after her. Prez came in and told me she would be back and I need to trust him.

CHAPTER 19

CLAIRE

2 Months later

"Hey Uncle Graham how are things? What can I do you for?" All I can think is don't ask about Princess. I don't know where she is. I've tried everything to find her.

"My Princess tells me she isn't coming back. Is this true? And what is being done with Danny and this other fucker?"

Heaving a deep breath I say "I can't find her she was in contact 2 months ago when she arrived at a hotel that's all I've heard from her. I don't know what way she headed. And as for Danny and fuckhead they are still in the think tank. The money is gone. But they are working with someone else other than their own club we need to know who and how to neutralize the possible threat."

"Princess is in Florida at the moment. I speak to her daily. Now I want to know why, when I video chatted with her she has a scar running down her face and her hand and arm are the same? And no one told ME A FUCKING THING!? "

"SHIT I didn't know, all I was told from her was she was fine. I haven't reviewed the tape of what happened but the slut involved is out. And I will send the guys to get her. Tonight. Sorry Uncle Graham I dropped the ball on this one I should have had a better eye on her."

Silence on the other end of the phone does not bode well. "She is working at a bar which I know is run by bikers. So I would advise you move your ass and you go get her. I've already sent Chris he should be there today or tomorrow morning. Enjoy working with him as he is pissed that he has to do YOUR job. If he gets to her first, I can assure you he won't leave the USA for the next year. At least! That man has loved her for the last year. But has kept his distance, due to me. I'm not there Claire. He will keep her wrapped in cotton wool and keep her pure not allow her to live her life or learn what she must. I trusted you Angel thinking you would teach her what she needs to know. You failed and he was my only man available to get her safe. Get your ass to Florida now! " he hangs up with a click.

I'm not sure whether to be pissed at myself, Princess, that fucking whore or Demon. Better add that Chris fucker in the mix as well just for good measure. Walking towards my room I see Demon with a club whore from behind and she turns to talk to him and its Candy wtf? Why is she back? She is the one who made Princess run, why would anyone let her back? Nope not dealing with this I need to haul ass to Florida, holiday for the kids for the weekend. Getting to my room I hear Rage come down the hall "Hey sexy how did your call go?"

"Pftt don't ask just help pack for Florida for the weekend we are going to pick up Princess. And possibly a fuckhead too."

" OK I will let our brothers there know, we are coming. Take it the call wasn't a good one."

"No it wasn't I got my ass reemed. Why have I not been told what happened that day? Did you know she has a scar on her face and her hand and arm? Does no one think I should have known that little tidbit!? And why is Candy back?"

Rage looks at me sheepishly and I just know I'm not going to like this answer "Well babe I didn't think that you should know. You have had enough on your plate with downstairs and the kids and this pregnancy. We were looking for her. I knew she was hurt just not how badly. And Candy has been seeing Demon for about two weeks. Not our business babe."

My jaw feels like its hit the floor."Don't bother packing. Me and the kids will go ourselves. I'm going to go take care of my cousin like I should have done months ago. Stay clear of me for a while or I will cut your cock off" I ground out through my teeth. Turning I walk out of my room hearing "Fucking idiot!" From Rage.

Heading out the clubhouse I hear "Bye bye bitch" from Candy. Oh I will deal with her ass when I'm back. I'm going to pick up my kids and get on a flight.

ONE DAY LATER

Seeing Princess walk into the bar, me and the kids head into the bar. I step up to the bar and say "Hi Princess. Ready to come back yet? I know Chris is here but has he found you yet? "

She turns so quickly I'm amazed she doesn't have a crick in her neck. "Fuck! Why are you here Angel? If dad sent you, tell him I will phone him and kick his ass over the phone later. I'm not a child anymore. I have enough on my plate without adding you and that fucking clubs shit on me too. Go back home!"

"No"

"What? No what? Actually don't answer that. I'm going back to work. "

OK so she's pissed. But her poor face! It looks like a jagged line from her cheek bone to just above her jaw. That bitch Candy is going to pay. Nonchalantly I mention Demon. "OK you don't want to go back. I wouldn't if I were you either, will be hard seeing Demon and Candy together. He's about to make her his Old Lady any day now." That's when I see her fire. Oh someone's going to have her wrath and it ain't going to be me. I'm just going to have a box of popcorn and enjoy the fuckin show.

"Pardon? Let me say to Dev that I'm going back home for a few months then I will, and I fuckin mean it Angel, I will be back here. "

I've still got it ! Small seed and it grows and grows until she comes out her shell and shows who she really is. A major bitch and I'm damn proud to say she is my family.

She heads off to talk to whoever Dev is. I look around us to see what this place is about. And see a bunch of bikers staring at me. All of them are massive and around mid 20s and late 40s. There's about 20 of them give or take. And they are all wearing a scowl on their faces. What did I do now. What could I have possibly done in the whole 10 minutes I have been here? Turning my face to the kids I tell them to take a seat and I will get them a juice. "Mum is Princess coming home today?" Peter asks while Ava asks "Why are those men staring at us? Its a bit creepy mum."

Just as I'm about to answer a voice dripping in gruffness that sounds like the guy must be yummy. As it sends a shiver down my spine says " I can answer that one darlin'. Those men are part of this club and are wondering why a pregnant Old Lady who belongs to a brother is miles from home with her kids in tow without said brother, is here asking my little Princess to go home. She will go back with you to sort this shit storm up, then, she will come home with me. Do we understand each other darlin' ? I have already laid claim to her, she agreed. End of fuckin story. "

Holding on to the temper by a thread I lift my head and answering with "Why I'm here without my ol man is none of your concern pal. If she is happy here you best be ready to deal with not only her father but the man he has sent, who I am actually surprised he isn't here already."

Taking a good look at this guy. I see first and foremost his patch. 'President' he must be around 6ft 9 and muscles on top of muscles. Jesus she definitely upgraded from Demon. His face has a scar running from just above his lip on his left side to just in front of his ear. It doesn't look like a straight line. It looks like someone deliberately made that scar and not like a swipe of a knife. Someone took their time. He has deep blue eyes black hair tied behind his head and a red bandana around his head. He looks kind of scary but at the same time is probably good to Princess. But alas she will need to deal with and tell Demon what the fuck is going on. And to confront that skanky whore back home. She can't allow her to win. That's not our families way never has been never will be.

Princess appears at the mans side. She is wearing a pair of tight ass hugging jeans in light blue with tears on the thighs and a simple black T-shirt with the club insignia on it. She pulls on a property of Devil cut on. And that makes me smile. She is showing not only everyone that she is his Old Lady but me that she will not back down from me or the club. "Ready when you are handsome. Are we on your bike or are we going in the plane?"

"Plane baby. We will hire a car while we are there. Slice and Range will be accompanying us as well. They have already sent that Chris guy home. He won't be back you need to phone your dad make him back off babe." His eyes soften as he looks down at her. He wraps his arm around her and whispers something in her ear that makes her smile and kiss him. This is a kiss that makes me even shift in uncomfortableness. I mean she is my cousin I really don't need to see this shit like ever!

"OK people let's go. Times a wasting and all that PDA is something neither me nor my kids need to see. Book your flights and let's go."

"Phone your dad Princess. We can wait for that. Let him know what is going on. He deserves to know my little Princess, everything." Devil says in an understanding voice.

What? What does that mean? Yet again out of the loop, that's beginning to seriously piss me off.

Watching Princess walk away to the back of the bar. I stand here wondering if I should follow or ask what he meant by "He deserves to know". Well best get this show on the road. I need food and a strawberry milkshake. Let's see what storm brings shall we?

The next day

Walking into the clubhouse I see Demon sitting in his booth (yes he named his own booth) with Candy. Knowing Princess is about to turn up I kind of want to tell Demon she is here and what's what, but seeing not only her smirk but his dirty look towards me. Let the fireworks begin. Seeing my man sitting with Teeth, Crank, Joker, Syco and Lucius I head to them. The all say hi and wonder where the kids are. "Ava is out with Katelyn and Peter is tinkering with Rage's old bike. Oh this will be fun!"

Princess walks in the club wearing tight as fuck black jeans a black spaghetti strap top with Devil's Princess in italic red writing and white 5 inch knee high boots. Pretty big ass statement right there, add in the Property of cutt and that's just a slap in the mother fuckin face! All eyes snap to her never mind the muscle on muscle man standing right beside her looking like he is ready to deliver pain to anyone who fucks with his Old Lady. Damn this really will be fun to watch! I'm like a kid on Christmas morning!

She scans the room spies her prey and grabs a glass and a cloth and walks over to us. "Hi all, Lucius you don't mind if I clean house with some skank do you? Oh I'm sure you know my old man. Devil. I want my revenge on that little skank over there. I will not allow some whore to damage me and take what was my place in this club and where I called my home for her own. I want blood for this Lucius and what better way than with a clean glass. Since she at least waited until I cleaned the glass. Once this has been done I will collect my things spend a day here for my man and then we will leave and I will only return when my man says I've to come here with him. "

Lucius looks at her with an awed respect. He looks at devil and says " OK Princess floors all yours. No need to rush off after though. Sit and visit with us."

Watching her walk with purpose toward Candy and Demon, all the while wiping the glass in her glass. Devil is still standing beside our table, with a smirk on his face, which makes the scar scrunch up and that's when I see it resembles an L on its side. What the fuck happened to him? Turning to see what is happening with Princess. I can see all eyes are on her, don't blame them to be honest she is a stunner. Demon really is a moron, he gave up perfection for slutville. As I said moron.

She finishes cleaning that bloody glass, sits it in the middle of the table with a clank and waits for both sets of eye to be on her and smiles while saying "Hey darlin, miss me? I have a few things to say then I will leave." Candy starts laughing and snarls "You don't belong here just like I told you. How's the face? Looks better than the original version"

Just as she is about to turn to Demon, Princess grabs her arm and slams it on the table. "I wasn't fuckin finished bitch. Face is fine as it's a part of why I have my ol man. But yours is just about to see how much he really is your ol man. Let's see if he sticks with you after this" She grits through her teeth as she slams that glass into her arm, shattering it into her left arm then taking the base of the glass and dragging it over her face from cheek to ear. "Hurts doesn't it ? Not once has Demon moved. What do you think that means? Huh? Enjoy each other you both deserve each other and more" Turning to Demon she looks at him like he is a piece of shit under her shoe and says " And I thought you would have learned with your first Old Lady. Guess I was wrong. Goodbye Demon."

"Ha little girl, Candy will obliterate you when she is ready. And no doubt it won't be long. I will happily have a front row seat to that shit. Don't think you are as protected as you think." Demon snarls at her while taking a step towards her. At that I stand up, slide one of my flat blades out of my belt and throw. Hearing the whistle through the air, then the thump as it hits its mark in his right hand, is satisfying to say the least. "Fuck sake Claire! Why? What did you think I was going to do ? You stupid bitch!" Demon shouts at me.

"You threatened Princess, not in front of me you don't, she is family. You are not. Step back or the next is lower. Your choice asshole!"

Giving me a look of death, he spits "Bitch you better stay away from me. Your Uncle may have us over a barrel with shit but, Candy is right same with the rest of these sluts. You are a fuckin waste to Rage. As soon as he realizes this shit you and your fuckin cunt of kids will be gone and good riddance." He walks out of the club carrying Candy. I've still got my eyebrows in my forehead in shock. Hearing a struggle behind me I turn to see, Rage being held around the arms by Syco and Lucius. Well I guess he wasn't happy with that.

Sitting down he wraps me in his arms and whispers "Angel that fucker is a walking dead man. You are never a waste to me. You and the kids are my everything. Certainly never knew I needed you until I had you and you are never leaving me nor will I leave you. You are MINE! My Old Lady ! MY woman! Love you always baby! Forget what he said. He doesn't know know shit. Calm down and think of our little girl. " He is right. I need to stay calm for the kids. And my little girl in my womb.

Looking across the table I notice Princess wrapped in Devil's arms. She seems happy, but I need to know how they met, how long they have been together. Yeah I'm nosey but I don't give a shit.

CHAPTER 20

ANGEL

After Princess, Devil and the rest of his chapter left. There was a giant meeting minus Demon. He was being stripped of his colours after what he did. They just had to find him and his slut. It's not like we didn't have enough to deal with. It was also decided to kill Moss, and send a message to whoever the others in with him are. Don't fuck with the club.

After 3 months it was getting close to my due date. I didn't want to deal with Danny while I was pregnant. I wanted to be able to have my child and have Uncle Graham here when he was dealt with. I needed a few weeks of peace, no stress for Ella Belle to arrive. No I didn't name her. Rage did, I just agreed. Well it is a nice name, I just hope it suits her when she is born. Ava and Peter are doing great in school, but are always asking after Princess. We haven't spoken since she was here and I never got the answers to my questions. I would be nice to be told what the fuck happened. But she won't tell me. Or at least not right now. I have 3 weeks until due date and I have everything ready. Rage has went totally over board but its his first time being a dad, so can't really blame him. The club are still selling my Uncles drugs and guns. I'm not part of that, still tattooing, although I'm on maternity leave. I've got to the point now where I want my baby girl out. 3weeks and she will be here. That all I can think.

Driving through town for some food shopping, well I say food shopping more like someone ate my ice cream and I needed to drag my ass to get some. Walking around the store I'm stopped when Demon and Candy grab onto my cart. "Well if it isn't the bitch! Where is your ol man? Not here by the looks of things. "

Rolling my eyes I return with "Obviously dickless ! What do you want? Or have you stopped me to hand me your cutt? If so, hand it over and fuck off. Standing near that walking std gives me hives. "

Said walking std slaps me across the face! Really?! Hell fuckin no! Just as I take a step forward my waters burst. No no no not here not in front of these fuckers!

"Shit, Angel. Let's get you to the hospital. I will phone Rage."

Eh? What?

"Candy go to the car. Now!"

"Why are you helping this bitch. We were going to kidnap her and wait until she gave birth then sell the baby back to Rage then kill this bitch!" She moans in a high pitch voice.

At that I feel a giant contraction and lash out at this slut. Knocking her out in one punch. Demon turns open mouthed and starts laughing.

"That was fuckin perfect Angel. Now let's get my Neice born. Wait you're early. Shit come on."

" What the fuck is going on? You aren't part of the club anymore. Why should I trust you?"

Sighing he shakes his head saying "Angel you won't like this. What was said and done at the club that day was a set up. I have alot to tell you and the club about what's been happening. But the club decided we needed someone to either follow Candy or be her ol man and follow her lead. There's a lot of shit you don't and won't know especially this. Just know I wasn't ever out of my club. Now can we please get you to the hospital."

Gritting my teeth through the pain I nod my head. Getting into the car during a contraction is a bitch and a half. Having a man telling me to breathe is downright fucking annoying. I'm not exactly holding my bloody breath am I?!

It took 20 minutes to get to the hospital and I was about due to kill Demon within 4 of those minutes. "How are you? Are you OK? Do I need to stop? Do you need to push? Is she coming out of your pussy right now? Do you want me to phone ahead? " Argh shut the fuck up!!! I ignored him all the way.

The guys had phoned to say they had picked up Candy and had her in the cage. And that Rage and Lucius would meet us at the hospital.

Going in the doors I walk up to the reception and say my name and that I'm 3 weeks early. Giving my doctors name I'm taken to a room, hooked up to every available machine it seems. I'm getting worried with all these things hooked to me. As a midwife and my doctor walk in they ask how I am. "I'm sore but why am I on all these machines. What's wrong?"

"Nothing is wrong its just precaution. As you are early and you are 6cm dilated, this is going quick so we will monitor you until you are around 9cm and get you ready for birth. Do you want any pain relief?"

I sigh in relief. "Just gas and air will do. Its all I have ever taken with my kids. If someone could pass my phone so I can make sure someone picks my kids up from school though I would be thankful."

Giving me my phone they both leave the room. Just as Teeth's phone rings, Rage and Lucius walk through the door. I smile as I see Rage looks like he is about to faint. "Won't be long babe and you will be holding her in your arms. Can someone get me some ice please?"

"Hello, what's up Mama? Shouldn't you be pushing her out of your pussy yet? " Oh I am going to slap him when I get out of here!

"Asshole do me a favor?"

"Already picking the kids up Mama! Just you bring my other Neice into the world. Don't worry about a thing." And he hangs up. Fucker!

Feeling one hell of a contraction, I shout for someone to get the doctor. Not 2 minutes later he appears. "Let's see how you are doing, shall we? Deep breath for me Claire." Taking a deep breath just as he checks how far I am. He smiles saying I'm at 9cm and ready to get her out.

2 hours later I am holding my Ella Marie. She really didn't look like an Elle Belle. She has a full head of light brown hair. Big blue eyes and a cute as hell

button nose. She came quietly into the world a healthy 8lb 3oz. She loves her bottle so far. And her daddy is already wrapped around her finger. He hasn't stopped smiling and looking at her. Smitten is what he is. So is Lucius. Granddad Lucius came in the room with a babygrow in bright pink with "Club Princess" written on it in white.

Wakening from a nap I see Ava and Peter sitting at the side of me on the bed looking at Ella Marie. Sitting up I cuddle them both. "I see you've met your little sister. How was school? Any homework?"

Ava rolls her eyes and says "Yes mum homework was done by both of us. School was good wasn't happy you didn't phone us though! But we came straight here when Uncle Teeth came and got us. How's mummy? You look tired, do you need more sleep? We can feed and change her if you want?"

Oh I can totally see she just wants to hold her. She may say she will change her but once she opens that nappy she will point blankly say she isn't changing dirty nappies ever. " Do you want to hold her? " Both sets of eyes light up. Taking that as a yes then. They both don't want to put her down. Sadly its feeding time for her then back to sleep. Just as I start undressing her Rage walks in the room with a giant teddy, a bunch of roses and 2 new phones. How long was I asleep? Jeez.

Kissing me on the head he looks at Ella Marie and dips down with a kiss on her head and smiles. He turns to the kids and hands them both a phone each. "Eh? What are you doing? They don't need phones."

Rage turns to me gives me a look "Babe I wanted to get them the newest phone so I did. I got you flowers and the biggest teddy for our newest Princess. Can you just let me spoil everyone for once?"

Huffing I stay silent. What exactly can I say to that? Nothing as I'm nearly in tears. He is so sweet when he isn't trying to be the big bad alpha.

After feeding Ella Marie the kids go with Rage and head home. Once Ella Marie is settled I go for what I know is going to be 3 hours sleep.

ANGEL

CHAPTER 21

RAGE

Walking out of this hospital the day after Angel gave birth to my daughter, heading home I couldn't be happier. Seeing my baby girl sleeping in her seat. I may have went Ott as I've got mirrors so I can see her. This is the best feeling in the world. I am officially a dad. In 2 months Danny will be dealt with and everything can go back to normal. Turning down the road to our house, I can't help the smile on my face. The old timers Old Ladies have made a spread for us coming home the kids are in the house waiting for us, and tomorrow, I marry my Angel. She doesn't know that yet though and the kids have kept this secret from her for the last month. Everything is sorted and we will be married at the clubhouse.

Getting in the house and settling our baby girl in the moses basket for a nap. My Angel says she is going to go see the kids and talk to them for a bit as she hasn't really saw them since she went into hospital. An hour later she comes down and cuddles up to me on the sofa and relaxes for a bit. "Babe would you do me a favor tomorrow? Go and get some pampering done. You deserve it after everything we have been through you deserve some pampering. The girls have it all set up. I will take the kids to the clubhouse with me to do some paperwork. "

Tiredly she replies "OK babe if you are sure. I could also do with some stuff for the house. I will get that while I'm out. Will I just meet you at the clubhouse?"

Smiling down at her I kiss her on the head and tell her yes.

Tomorrow I will be a married man.

Angel

After being up and down all night with Ella Marie I slept until 10am. Stretching I see a clothing bag hung up on the door with a note saying "Open me", getting up I walk over and do as the note says. I stand there with my mouth agape. It's a cream summer dress. Why the hell would he get me this? Sure as fate it has a note " Wear me today".

Doing as it says, hey I can play whatever game he wants me to, putting it on I even pretty my hair up. Taking my time to put curls in it. I look pretty good just make up and then I will head into town to get pampered and some food for the house.

Getting into town and going to the nail salon. I'm met at the door by Lizzy who is one of the guys ol ladies. She has a smile wide and says "You're early. What do you want done? Something simple or something different?"

"Simple just give me white with red flowers please Lizzy. So what are you doing other than my nails? Once I'm done here I'm going for some shopping then back to the clubhouse to get my babies."

After 2 hours of hand and feet pampering she hands me a box. "What's this?"

She has a giant grin and giggles out "Rage said its all part of your pamper day. Enjoy it. He is a great man hun you couldn't have done any better than him." Turning she goes out the front for a smoke.

Opening the box I'm stunned to see a smaller box, as well as a pair of 3inch heeled cream patent shoes that are utterly gorgeous. Opening the smaller box I start to cry. There's a note that says

You are invited to the wedding of

Claire 'Angel' Miller

And

Ryan 'Rage' Silver

At the Clubhouse at the time of

3pm

He wants to marry me! Checking the time and seeing I still have an hour left that gives me 30 minutes to touch up my make up.

Half an hour later I'm heading to the club with butterflies in my stomach. I am actually nervous. I have no knives on me at all. I feel naked but in a good way. 15 minutes later I'm pulling into the clubhouse. Walking through the doors the kids are waiting for me looking so dapper. Ava is in a light blue dress but it has the club insignia on the back marking her as a club brat. Peter is in a 5 piece navy blue suit with light blue tie that looks like he has been pulling on it. Walking up to him I say "Are you ready to give your mum away baby boy?"

He nods his head and allows me to sort his tie. Turning to Ava I smile and need to keep the tears at bay "My big grown girl. You are gorgeous. I love you both so much. Are you both OK with this? A hundred percent sure?"

Looking at each other they smile and nod their heads. "Mum he loves you, you love him. You're happy mum and that makes us happy, plus he is kinda awesome." Ava says with a smile a mile wide.

"Let's get me married then. Show me the way baby girl." With that she turns a CD on that plays Scott Brown - Rock You Softly. My kids know me too well.

Ava turns to me gives me a kiss on my cheek and leads the way. Peter and I wait a minute before following her to the door. Once she is about half way down the seated area that is covered in white Lillie's and pink roses. Peter pulls me down and whispers " I love you mum. Always and forever." Trying my hardest not to cry. I say "I love you too baby boy forever and always" Peter starts to walk and its killing me not to run to Rage. As I look at him in his suit exactly the same as Peter's, he is so handsome. Ruggedly so. His muscles look like they are about to burst out of that suit. I start to giggle as I see its not a normal suit, its a shirt tie jacket but this jacket is leather and has his patch as well as my name under it. Standing in front of him, I turn to Peter and give him a kiss on the head and nod at him.

After the ceremony which I tried my hardest not to cry. Didn't succeed. We take an hour to ourselves just to be husband and wife. "I love you Rage. I'm just sorry that we can't consummate this marriage. Well I can't have anything but you certainly can" with that I drop to my knees and proceed to take his thick hard length out and stroke it slowly. Looking up his eyes are locked on me. Slowly running my tongue around the head, I wrap my lips around his thick cock and slide him fully into my mouth. Slowly sucking him I feel him twitch. Humming a silly tune as I suck his massive cock. I can feel he won't be long until I taste his cum. And not 3 minutes later he explodes in my mouth and I swallow it all. I hate the taste of cum. Just shows how much I love him as he knows I hate the taste of it.

CHAPTER 22

RAGE

3 months later

We are having a patch in party. 2 of 4 prospects are patching in to the club tonight. We have the other 2 down in the cage watching our prisoner's. If they don't fuck this up they will be patched in this week. But these guys have been here for a full year and have been through some amount of shit for us.

Looking at the bar I see my Old Lady, my wife the mother of my kids. Yes I said kids, officially and legally I adopted the kids a month ago. Peter will no doubt be a part of the club, as Lucius has taken him under his wing and Ava, well she's always going to be a club brat. She is always talking about boys and I am always chasing them away. Until one has the balls to stand up to me they won't get near her. She understands where I am coming from but, wow, does she have her mothers temper. She's a little ball of terror when she kicks off. And Ella Marie is growing into her own. She used to be so quiet, not so much now. She has a serious set of lungs on her. The only person she settles for is Teeth for some strange reason. The second she is in his arms she is silent. The kids are currently with Teeth and his new woman, Stephanie. She is quiet, shy and reserved. There's a story there as she never leaves the club.

Seeing Lucius searching the club until his eyes land on me. He tilts his head towards his office, and I just know I'm not going to like this.

"What's up Pres?"

Shaking his head he replies "We have a fucking major problem. Both Candy and Danny are gone. One prospect dead and the other missing. Assumed to have gotten the fucking cunts out. We have to tell Angel and the brothers. I'm expecting an explosion from Angel. I've sent a few of the brothers out to search. They couldn't have gotten far. But we don't know what they are driving. Go get Angel we will talk first, then let the other charters know to be on the lookout."

"Shit! How the fuck did they get past us? Surely someone saw them!? Angel is going to blow up at this. So will her Uncle! This is a fucking shit storm of epic fucking proportions Pres. " heading out to go get Angel I see her at the bar with a beer in hand. Shit!

"Babe, Pres needs you in the office its important. "

"OK sexy, will be there right now." She smiles at me. Yeah that's going to be the last smile I see tonight. So much for fucking her since before Ella Marie was born. I will be lucky if I even see my bed tonight.

Walking in the door, Pres is sitting behind his desk looking downright pissed off. And I am the same. Looking between us she realizes something is seriously wrong.

"What's happened? Who died?"

"Sit down Angel. A prospect was killed on our property tonight and a couple of people have disappeared along with another prospect. It was Candy and Danny who have disappeared. I've sent a search party out, but we need to inform the brothers and then the charters around. We need you to have a level head." Pres explains calmly.

I didn't even get to 3 in my count before she blew. "Are you fucking shitting me right now? How the fuck did this happen. Someone fuckin answer that! How did they get past us all? How was that possible with a clubhouse of brothers?"

"We will find out. But we are on lockdown. Check the kids, although I know they will be OK as they are with Teeth and Stephanie. But just for all of our peace of mind, check please. " Lucius orders her. Angel leaves with a temper in her step.

"Shit!" I grunt out.

ANGEL

After checking on the kids, I phone Uncle Graham. I got straight to the point and tell him what's happened. He ain't pleased not in the slightest. Neither am I! I knew I should have killed him when he first arrived here. We still don't know who he was working with.

What the fuck am I to do? Hunt for them again I guess. My phone pings with a text

Unknown: Bitch you will pay. I'm going to see the tower crumble and laugh as you all go to hell!!!

Me: Whoever you are I will be there long after you are

There's no reply but out of instinct I text Princess

Me: Fuck nugget 1 and 2 escaped. Keep an eye out. Stay safe please. Lucius will phone Devil. Love you xx

Princess: Hear ye loud and clear cousin. Eyes on alert. Devil read the text and is waiting on the call from Lucius. Club going on lockdown as we speak. Love you too give the kids a kiss and say hi to Rage. Xxx

At least I know everything will be fine with her. One less problem to worry about.

Now to find these little fuckers.

DANNY

Little cow doesn't know who she is messing with. I can't wait until she finds out. Meeting up with Craig 3 towns over we make our plan for the Princess and getting her back where her whore ass belongs!

The End

Thank you for reading. This book is the first in a series. The next book is about Princess and Devil. The first chapter is included on the next page. Enjoy.

PRINCESS

CHAPTER 1

Staring at the bar lost in my thoughts. My scar is itchy and I know not to scratch so I'm trying to keep my hands busy by cleaning glasses. Feeling strong arms surround me, I smile knowing its my Devil. We didn't start off great to be honest, he was being my ol man to protect me. It wasn't until we walked into Angels club that he realized he wouldn't and couldn't allow anything to happen to me. It was a simple agreement. He protected me and I lived at his house to be basically his live in maid. And I was fine with that until the first time I saw him have a nightmare.

That was the scariest thing I have ever seen. This big brute of a man screaming and roaring in his sleep made my heart break for him. I tried to wake him and all that succeeded in doing was having me be bear hugged and strangely calming him. The next night the same thing happened. This happened nightly for about a week. And every night my heart broke for him. In the mornings he was nowhere around. I hated it ! I just wanted him to open up.

Yeah cos that's what I do. I never told him what happened. He overheard a conversation with my dad, he then demanded to know who he was. Explaining who and what my father was. Was difficult. I knew that Angels husbands club dealt with my father but I wasn't sure what Devil knew. In the end I took a leap and told him everything. It took a fair few drinks, but in the end it all and I mean all came tumbling out. He held me that night promising me he would never leave my side. He has kept his promise. About three weeks later I was seriously drunk. And told him how handsome he was. That night I told him that I wanted to be with him for real, the next week we became a couple. I know I should explain a hell of a lot more and I will but back to the arms around me.

"What's wrong Princess? What's with the face? Where's my smile?" He asks while running running his hands over my belly.

"Nothing Devil. Just wishing I could go to bed and cuddle. Kind of missing my dad, I haven't seen him in a year. Talking on the phone isn't helping. I know he is dealing with a lot but, well I thought, I thought he would want to come see me. Have a break, come see his only child. God, I sound like a spoiled brat. Sorry babe I will shut up now."

Turning me in his strong arms he smiles at me and whispers "Come to bed I will help take all these upsetting thoughts out of your head."

Smiling I walk away from him towards our room and turn my head and say "Only if you spank me like you did last night big boy. Oh and do that thing with your tongue."

He does this amazing thing where he swirls his tongue while plunging it deep within me. Nothing compares to it, well except maybe his cock. But that thing I have named 'Beast' and a beast it is. He is thick and seriously long. If he would actually allow me to measure it, I'm positive it would be about 11 inches. Devil likes to be rough in bed, and I mean rough. He loves to spank, tie my hair round his fist while he fucks me from behind. He ties me up in some amazing ways. They make me squirt and I swear the first few times it felt like I was peeing.

"Oh Princess, you want it hard tonight don't you. I will fuck you til you pass out. And you will love every second of it. GET UPSTAIRS NOW!" He snarls with that look in his eyes that say I'm going to have a shit load of sex tonight. Just what I need.

Running upstairs I pass Sparky, one of the brothers who is one of my good friends at the club. He was the first to see me for me and not wince at my scar. Nodding at him, he smirks knowing exactly what is going to be happening. He walked in when I was tied in a very sexual way. Devil had me spread wide and wanton, and Sparky walked in to tell Devil something and promptly walked back out the door with his eyes wide as saucer's. Wasn't funny at the time, but fuck it is now. Running into the room I slam it shut and hit the lock home. I know I will be punished but I love when he smacks my bum.

Hearing him coming down the hall, just as he gets to the door his phone rings. Oh, he better not answer that. Of bloody course he does! Listening to his conversation through the door, I just know he isn't coming in to play. "We will be there in 10 minutes. Don't let him out of your sight prospect!" Well shit that doesn't sound very good.

He walks in the door and looks at me standing rigidly by the bed, he knows I know he needs to go. This comes with the territory of being Pres of the club.

"Well well well my Princess seems we have a visitor. Now I'm going to fuck you quickly right now to take the edge off both of our needs. You have not to make a sound , do you understand? Not one peep! Or I stop!"

Nodding my head in total agreement. He spins me around, flicks my skirt up and rips my panties off. Bending me over our queen size bed until my face is pressed against the mattress, he slams his cock in me hard and unyieldingly. He is like a battering ram. I know I will be deliciously sore for the rest of the night. He is relentless in his rutting. I love when he is like this as it gets me off so much faster. He leans forward to lay across my back and bites my shoulder until I grunt from the pleasure pain, and I know I made a noise. I'm just hoping he either didn't hear it or he is too far gone. But no my ass is slapped hard! Biting my lip hard to stop from making a noise, he continues until we both come apart and I feel the warm splash of his cum hit my uterus.

"Fuck Princess, you squeeze my cock like a fucking vice. But you need to get dressed and out the door your dad is here."

"WHAT!? Fuck sake Devil! Move, dad won't like being kept waiting!" I screech at him trying to get a fresh pair of panties on. And rushing him out the door. What is dad doing here? He didn't phone! Surely he would have let me know that he was coming?

Walking into the main room of the club I see whores all over the place in complete undress. Arghhh he will be demanding I leave the second he speaks to me. Time to pull up the big girl panties and tell him I'm happy here.

Printed in Great Britain
by Amazon

18580692R00133